STORY CHAT

Online Literary Conversations

SERIES OF SHORT STORIES AND RUMINATIONS

Introduction to "Story Chat"

To chat is to talk in an informal and familiar manner or have online discussions in a chat room. **Story Chat** is a series of short stories and great conversations that were published first on my blog.

I want to thank each of the contributing authors for contributing their excellent stories, as well as all the bloggers who commented on them.

Hugh W. Roberts from England

Cathy Cade from England

Anne Goodwin from England

Geoff Le Pard from England

Doug Jacquier from Australia

Anne Stormont from Scotland

Debbie Harris from Australia

Gary A. Wilson from the United States

Wendy Fletcher from England

K.L. Caley from England

Yvette Prior from the United States

Charli Mills from the United States

Phillip Cumberland from England

Gloria McBreen from Ireland

Amazingly, the bloggers who commented would share vulnerable, deeply personal experiences that related to the story. They compared the author's short story to famous stories, movies, and television series that the story made them remember. They argued with each other about what they thought the author meant or what should have happened. They offered advice and sometimes argued about that. Most of all, they praised the brave author for stepping out and publishing their work for everyone to discuss. **Story Chat** is living proof that stories take on a life of their own when you add readers.

Spelling and punctuation reflect the norms of the countries of the bloggers who participated in both the stories and the comments. Since I do not know the rules of grammar in other countries, I did little, if any, editing of the stories and the comments.

Comments about the experience by Story Chatters

💬 "I loved not only reading brand-new stories, but the interaction between readers was also great. The feedback is amazing. It's like having lots of Beta readers for a story you've written."

💬 "There was an excellent mixture of genres."

💬 "The balance is perfect. There has been a good mixture of male and female writers from all over the world."

💬 "I'd suggest keeping it to fiction and opening another **Story Chat** for non-fiction (if you go down that route)."

Thank you to all the authors who have contributed and to those bloggers who took the time to read the stories and comment. Now that you know how it all began and progressed, let's get on with the stories.

Chapter One:
"The People under the Stairs"

BY HUGH W. ROBERTS

Thank goodness they had gone. She'd spent 30 years trying to get rid of them, and they chose to go now, a week before she moved to a new home?

Raising her hands in the air, Gloria celebrated, knowing she'd beaten them. It must have been the leftover Stilton cheese from Christmas she'd placed under the stairs that had finally driven them out.

Now, with only a week to go before she moved to the residential home that catered for people with the early onset of dementia, she could finally get started on sorting out 30 years of clutter.

Thirty years of disturbed sleep because of the people under the stairs had taken its toll on Gloria. Rather than begin sorting out clutter, she could have comfortably sat in her favourite armchair and taken a nap. The packing could wait until tomorrow, or somebody else could do it.

***

The following morning, Gloria awoke from the best night's sleep she'd had since the night of her honeymoon. Throwing back the bedcovers, she made her way downstairs to make the first cuppa of the day.

Just as she walked past the door that led to the stairs, Gloria came to a grinding halt. Was that a noise she'd heard coming from behind the door, or was it her imagination?

"Oh, I do hope you're back," sighed Gloria as she placed her hand on the door handle. "I'm going to countdown from three. If you're not in there, they'll be in trouble. Three, four, two... Whoosh!"

Nothing but darkness and the faint smell of cheese met Gloria. She felt slightly disappointed that nobody was there. A sudden noise from upstairs startled her, forcing her to close the door quickly.

'Gloria? Is that you?" came a muffled, familiar voice from above her.

"You're my little secret. My first job of the day after my morning cuppa will be to clear out this cupboard; your home," Gloria told herself.

***

By the day of the move, Gloria had become a little depressed. How could the people from under the stairs have left her? They may have given her 30 years of disturbed sleep, but they were her best friends. She should never have made them go.

"Come on," said a familiar voice of a man she didn't recognise. "It's time to go. Do you want to take a final look around the house before we go?"

Shaking her head, Gloria shed a few tears. Not only was she leaving behind 30 years of memories, but leaving behind 30 years of living with the people from under the stairs.

***

On the first night in her new home, Gloria woke to the sound of scratching coming from under her bed. Were they back? The people from under the stairs, were they back?

As she watched the duvet cover slowly disappear down the bed, revealing the bodies of her and a man who looked familiar, Gloria knew they were back.

Discussion

LIESBET: "Luckily, we don't have stairs in our camper van! And luckily, we were camped at a quiet location over Halloween. Great story, Hugh. I cannot imagine Gloria having dementia for thirty years, so she must have an incredible imagination."

TERRI:"...Gloria's dementia fueling her ghosts under the stairs, especially since she sees herself. Just vague enough, though, to make you wonder, though! Reminds me a little of the movie The Others (2001) with Nicole Kidman, thinking she and her kids were haunted by ghosts when in reality they were the ghosts!"

MR. OHHH: "Maybe she and those under the stairs plan to help those suffering from dementia cross over. Like she helped her husband years ago."

DIANA: "Apparently, she carries a love-hate relationship with the people under the stairs. I see them as her alter ego, her bad side, maybe even having murdered her husband some years ago._The element of dementia complicates reality... The unreliable narrator was a great addition to the story."

HUGH: "My mother had dementia, and some of the elements of this story were what I picked up from her. I often thought that she seemed to be living in a book, yet other times, I wasn't quite sure what she was saying was true or just what dementia was showing her.

My mother died at the age of 78. We first noticed the signs of dementia when she was in her early 70s, so she went through the different stages of the condition at a slow rate.

It was heartbreaking watching what I can only describe as something else taking over her body. The worst part for me was when she could not remember who I was."

Chapter Two: "Jenny's Bumpy Start"

BY MARSHA INGRAO

Sandy Lassiter looked over at Jenny and mouthed the words, "Behind you," then looked down at her paper as if her eyes were filled with iron filings and her desk was a magnet.

Jenny looked around the room. The teacher had stepped out of the room. Jenny Hatfield did not need to look around to know that Sandy meant Jeremy Crawford. He had been poking her in the back with his pencil all morning. All the kids quickly looked away as she tried to make eye contact.

Only one ally in this room, and Sandy was obviously not popular with the other kids. As usual, being the new kid at school was already off to a bumpy start.

Jeremy stood and loomed over her, staring down at her paper. "You think you are so smart, don't you, Nerd?" He grabbed her paper and stuck it in his math book.

"You'd better hope I'm smart if you're going to copy all my answers." Jenny looked up, but didn't smile.

"What's wrong with your mouth? Did your dad punch you in the face?" Jeremy whispered loudly enough that other students around her looked up, then buried their noses right back into their books. He started laughing loudly enough that the teacher looked back into the room.

"Jeremy, what are you doing out of your seat?" Mrs. Miller called from the door. "Sit down and don't let me see you get up until I tell you to."

"Yes, Ma'am." The thud when he sat down shook the floor.

"You're ugly, new girl," he whispered again, leaning forward in his seat.

"That's your opinion. You are a bully, Jeremy Crawford. Didn't anyone ever teach you how to make friends?" she hissed without turning around.

Jenny knew she had to be strong. She couldn't ignore him, threaten him, insult him back, or even tell the teacher. Many others before Jeremy had asked her that question about her face before. Sometimes she answered, and sometimes she didn't.

"Like I would want to be friends with you, Freak. Here's two cents. Go buy yourself a new smile. You need one."

Jeremy threw two pennies on her desk and laughed as they slid to the floor. Jenny leaned over to pull out her binder from under her desk, ignoring Jeremy as best she could. Her grandmother always told her to be friendly if she wanted to have friends, but she didn't want this misfit as a friend.

Jeremy's thick hair rested on his shoulders and looked and smelled like he had not washed it all week. Like a mangy stray dog, his smile chock full of crooked yellow teeth looked more menacing than friendly, and Jenny didn't want to get close enough to smell his breath. She certainly did not feel like giving him a smile, even a crooked one.

She put the two pennies in her pants pocket and wished for the millionth time that she was back with her friends in Portland rather than God-forsaken Latham School in the middle of nowhere. She quietly placed her binder on her desk, opened it, took out a new piece of paper, and began redoing her homework. Jeremy poked her again.

"I'm not afraid of you," Jenny mouthed. She already had three problems finished. Glancing behind her as she spoke, she could see that Jeremy hadn't even copied one of her problems yet.

Other kids stole glances at Jenny but quickly looked away, whispering among themselves.

"Oooh, I'm scared," Jeremy's voice must have carried beyond the classroom.

Mrs. Miller returned to the room and stood between Jenny and Jeremy. Jeremy pretended to work on his math homework. Mrs. Miller was so close Jenny could smell the soap on her hands.

"You'd better be scared of me, young man, and your homework better be started. You've only got three weeks before Christmas break to bring up that F in math," Mrs.

Miller said as she hammered a ruler on his desk near his fingers. "Now get to work."

Mrs. Miller clicked to the front of the room, her just-brightened red lips in a straight line. Jenny wasn't sure which one of them was the bigger bully as she heard the rivets on Jeremy's jeans scrape the wooden seat of his desk as he slumped down in his seat. Miss Magnolia at Grandview would never have told the entire class someone's bad grade, no matter how awful they were.

Jenny felt a slight breeze as she heard Jeremy's book slap the Formica top of the 1940s metal desk as he opened his book. Papers slid onto the floor and skittered toward her. Jeremy cursed. Mrs. Miller stood up as though she was going to come back over, then turned and wrote Jeremy's name on the board.

Jenny picked up the papers, kept hers, and gave the rest back to Jeremy. As he grabbed them and growled, she thought of an abused dog. Jenny wondered if Jeremy's parents were as mean to him as Mrs. Miller was.

Discussion

The discussion of "Jenny's Bumpy Start" moved quickly from a story about a new girl in school to a story about bullying.

ERIKA: "Your last paragraph hit the nail on the head. Blatant bullying used to be more obvious years ago. I think it likely still happens in new ways, such as cyberbullying or passive-aggressive ways."

Hugh: "It does make me wonder if Jeremy is being bullied at home, so he takes it out on somebody else. I see bullies as insecure, unhappy people who often don't want to help themselves, so they believe the whole world is against them.

Then, my thoughts moved to Jenny, and I wondered if she had been a bully at her previous school. Why? Because she seems to be handling Jeremy's bullying quite well."

CATHY: "I thought Jenny seemed to have a disfigurement, as she had been asked about her face before, but this wasn't clarified. Jenny seems a discerning girl to realise that the unprepossessing (unattractive) Jeremy isn't the only bully in the classroom, but it's likely she has been bullied before if she has a disfigurement. Since she misses her former school, she must have overcome any problems there and made friends. She will probably make friends here as well, given the time and her refusal to be provoked or intimidated – maybe even Jeremy."

ALEXIS: "I love how (this story) turns the tables on the idea that bullies are always the villain. I love how perceptive and kind Jenny is, not siding with the teacher because, although the teacher is trying to come to her defense, she's going about it all wrong. I love the unwritten complexity in Jeremy's character that we're able to sympathize with him despite his actions. I don't think Jenny is acting too old for her age, as some suggested; I've met some empathetic preteens. I also think it gives you the opportunity to explore how she got to be so mature."

Chapter Three:
"Out of Character"

BY CATHY CADE

Christmas ads had been filmed, and it was time for live appearances in department stores, handing out samples of Glint children's toothpaste as the jolly, padded, fur-clad Eva Beaver. Children seemed to like her. The feeling was not mutual.

They reminded her of school, which had sapped what little confidence she had to begin with. If her parents had not given her such a stupid name, maybe teachers—and later her classmates—would not have sniggered at the contrast it raised with this mousy, beige child with a mouthful of teeth. Her classwork was unexceptional. She was the last to be chosen for teams in sports lessons, but thanks to a sympathetic drama teacher, she participated in every school play. On stage, she could be anyone she wanted to be.

She had dreamed of an acting career. Once, she had believed her selection for the Glint toothpaste ads was a step nearer to her dream. But if that furry Eva Beaver costume sometimes felt like a straitjacket, at least she could pay the rent. Beggars with prominent front teeth and squeaky voices could not be choosy about their roles.

"I want a strawberry one. Don't like mango."

Eva rooted through her samples.

"Best I can do is raspberry."

She thrust it at him in a take-it-or-leave-it kind of way. Santa's elf shepherded the boy toward his father.

"I hope Santa brings you everything you want."

The father leered. "I wouldn't mind if he brought you down my chimney, love."

Santa's elf maintained a smile until she had bolted the scenery door behind them. She turned to Eva and mimed a gag response.

Eva smiled, "At least that's something I don't have to put up with in this outfit."

It was not something she encountered out of the costume either. Santa pushed back his hood to reveal a head as shiny as Humpty Dumpty's.

"That's it for today, bless 'em. Scott's in tomorrow. I'm off for a week."

"Lucky you," she said, taking off the furry hood with its round beaver ears and furry cheeks that covered hers. "I start at Spencer's in Warmington the day after tomorrow. I have precisely one child-free day."

"Oh, I won't be child-free," said Santa. "I'm at the children's hospice tomorrow. Then it is my kiddies' school Christmas fair and our church on the weekend. Busy month, December. Don't you love it?"

He headed for the cloakroom, humming Jingle Bells. The girl in an elf costume smiled.

"He's our nicest Santa. It has been good working with you, Eva. Have a great Christmas."

"You too," she said to the girl's back, not bothering to correct the name.

She even received mail addressed to Eva Troy. Out of the jumpsuit, she retrieved a large bag from behind the Christmas tree. Pulling out her coat and flat shoes, she stuffed the beaver suit into the bag and headed for home.

Another day, another grotto, another Santa,
and another brat.

"Santa doesn't exist. You're just some out-of-work actor."

"Ho, ho, ho," said Santa. "Very funny, young Joel. Collect your present from the elf through that door."

The door closed behind the boy.

"...Before I kick you through it," Santa recalled, he was not alone this week and glanced defiantly at Eva Beaver.

She smiled. "Don't you just hate the little... darlings?"

He relaxed. "You know, I really do sometimes." They gazed at the door in companionable silence. "All the time," they said in almost perfect unison.

An elf held back the curtain. "Eva Beaver is visiting Santa today. This is Shelley." The elf handed over her charge and returned to the queueing goblins.

Santa and Eva ate their sandwiches together in the staff room. She hardly noticed that his face was pinched and his hair receding. She laughed at his impersonations of spoiled princes and princesses and their powerless parents, pleased to have found someone who did not view her aversion to children as unnatural. She told him her dreams of acting, and he told her he would be rehearsing for pantomime over the weekend.

The next day, she wore a touch of mascara on her pale lashes. At closing time, she did what she could to brighten her mousy beige complexion in the cloakroom before she and Santa, whose real name was Ron, went for a drink.

On Thursday morning, she left her door open so that Mewsli could come in while she packed. The landlady's cat would greet her when she let herself in, as if he had been watching for her. He probably did the same with any lodger that stroked him, but she liked the camaraderie.

Tomorrow, she will take her suitcase to work and commute home afterward, but she might be too busy to pack tonight.

Thursday was a late-night opening. After closing, Ron walked her back to her digs. Mewsli came to greet them, and she bent to stroke the cat before starting up the stairs. At the sound of a yowl and a thump, she turned to see the Mewsli disappearing into the back of the house.

Ron raised his eyebrows as if to say, "What?"

"Actually, Ron… I have a headache. I'd better take a couple of pills and sleep it off, or I won't be fit for anything tomorrow."

He stood blankly before turning with thunder in his eyes and barely refrained from slamming the door.

The elves noticed the atmosphere the next day and were jollier than usual to liven it up.

Her friend Ginny worked her shifts in the pub whenever she worked as Eva Beavering. This week, she would cover for Ginny, who was in the chorus of Jack and the Beanstalk at the local theater.

Ginny wangled her for a free ticket for her and afterward took her backstage to meet the repertory group. She hoped to join them. Her initial nervousness was banished on coming face-to-rump with the back end of Daisy the cow. The front end smiled at her, clutching Daisy's head in his hands while the rear unzipped.

"Eva!"

Ron did not look pleased to see her. She restrained a giggle as she flung her taupe silk scarf across her shoulder. "It's Helen, actually," she said, taking Ginny's arm to move on.

Discussion

The reader's remarks turned outside the main characters to concern for the children who came to the mall to see Beaver Eva and Santa Ron. Parents not even mentioned in the story came under the readers' scrutiny and were given some cautionary advice.

DEEKSHA: "Parents are just blindly busy with the money race and hardly any time to look up at their children's activities. We grew up reading stories and exchanging storybooks with friends. Now children exchange video games."

PHIL: "Reading to children is one of the greatest gifts you can give them. It helps stimulate their imagination, helps them learn, and strengthens the bond between parent and child. A good book for older children I recommend is *The Silence* by Alison Bruce."

PATRICIA: "I assume this story is for teens/young adults/adults — a great target audience. Bring up some important points — parents do need to be mindful of their teens at the mall. There may be more behind Santa (Ron), as Eva intuitively realizes that she needs to be careful because she really doesn't know this Santa Ron and doesn't invite him into her apartment.

I like how she claims her real name at the end — that caught me off guard. She was on to better things. And it was clever to see Ron as the rump of Daisy the Cow—pun not intended. Not everyone is who they say they are."

Chapter Four:
"A Postcard from the Past"

BY ANNE GOODWIN

Ms Thompson – Ruth to her lover, colleagues, and friends – has set aside the afternoon to sort through old documents. Her retirement is some months away, but decommissioning thirty-five years' of professional paperwork requires a string of afternoons. A secretary could dispatch it in an hour, consigning it sheet by sheet to the shredder, but Ms Thompson feels obliged to examine every scrap. She's determined to disengage from social work as conscientiously as she began her career.

At the back of her filing cabinet, she discovers a buff-coloured file from the seventies. On removing the folder, a piece of glossed card slips out. The classic shot of five bridges across the Tyne reminds her of the case that shook her to the core.

The city was shabby when Diana, her client, enrolled at the university. But the nineties brought a concert hall and gallery to the quayside, spanned by a stylish sixth bridge. Françoise once suggested going there for a mini-break, but Ms Thompson – Ruth – demurred. Twenty years after closing the case, she'd have felt awkward bumping into the girl.

Ms Thompson flips the postcard over. The message is bland despite the spiky italics and green ink. *Settled in nicely. Enjoying my course. Making friends. Best wishes, Diana.* She'd scrawled the date above, perhaps to fill out the space: 15th October 1977. Ms Thompson isn't superstitious – although she sometimes checks her horoscope over lunch – but it makes her pause. The girl wrote the card twenty-seven years ago to the day.

She was surprised Diana chose to read psychology. Ms Thompson thought she'd go for something impersonal, like librarianship or maths. The social work role was redundant by that stage. Her task was completed when the girl left boarding school at eighteen. Yet Diana had sent the postcard. Ms Thompson had hung onto the file.

Now, scanning her notes from their first meeting three years before that, Ms Thompson feels a swell of sympathy for them both. Diana looked shell-shocked in her ill-fitting uniform, refusing to admit she was struggling. Ms Thompson, with her newly minted social work diploma, refused to admit she hadn't the skill or knowledge to put things right.

The headmaster hadn't either. That's why he'd called her in. But he had to balance Diana's needs against those of the school community. He'd restore order and avoid a scandal more easily with Diana out of the way.

The parents seemed oblivious: the mother was perplexed that the Social should interfere in her family's affairs. The father was distracted, gazing out the window when he wasn't ogling Ruth's breasts. The teenager was cagey and protective of her parents. Ms Thompson fumbled to find a resolution while, back at base, the upper echelons debated budgets and whether to involve the police.

A new school seemed the only option. A girls' boarding school where Diana could sever her ties to the past. Where bullies and gossip couldn't follow her. Where no one would know who she'd been before.

Ms Thompson had hoped to do more for her; hoped, over three years of boarding-school visits, Diana would confide her concerns. But the girl was unforthcoming. How did she cope with such a radical change alone?

Nowadays, there'd be compulsory counselling. Nowadays, her peers would approve. A girl in Diana's position would have team support from the beginning. A contemporary head teacher might make her head girl.

Ms Thompson stows the postcard in her handbag. A memento to take to the Dordogne. If she hadn't met Diana, would she be retiring to France?

She couldn't say if she'd helped the girl, but Diana had unwittingly helped her. Within the girl's silence about *her* transformation, Ms Thompson had nursed hers. If a teenager could risk ridicule to embrace her true identity, an adult had no excuse to deny hers, especially when the obstacles were relatively minor.

By the time Diana started her degree course, Ms Thompson had cropped her hair, got divorced, and met Françoise. She can only hope her former client is as happy with *her* choices as Ms Thompson is with hers.

Discussion

CHARLI: "Anne, if this short story was an excised scene from earlier drafts, why did it not make the cut? Curious revisionist wants to know!"

NORAH: "Like Charli, I'd also like to know why the scene was cut from the book, but I have to admit that, at the moment, I don't recall any conversations with Ms T in the novel. Perhaps I need a reminder. I can see that adding intrigue with another character may have distracted from Diana's own story. Perhaps Ms T. needs her own story."

ANNE: "She doesn't appear in the contemporary strand as she's part of Diana's past, but she's named in the first chapter when Diana remembers her. I thought of it this way before, but maybe minor characters like her are meant to be almost invisible because it isn't really her story. This was from a point where I thought I could tell Diana's story from multiple points of view."

The thread running through the stand-alone story was one of Ms. Thompson's feelings about herself, how she felt about her conduct as a social worker, and Diana's impact on her life.

D.: I think Ms. Thompson felt guilty and embarrassed about how she handled (or didn't handle) the case way back when. And maybe even chagrined in the face of Diana's courage and resolve when she had lesser issues to confront within herself. Maybe. It doesn't matter for this story; the questions are best left for readers to mull and not know. And they will be answered in the sequel, "Ms. Thompson Steps Out."

DOUG: "As both a recovering social worker (and someone who has taken to mining my past occasionally in my writing), I'm always confronted with whether the way I remember things is actually what happened or a polished/re-shaped version of how I felt or acted at the time. I sense that Ms T (and Ms G) may be struggling with the same question."

Chapter Five:
"Trophy Cabinet"

BY GEOFF LE PARD

Detective Inspector Triblane Pettimoron pinched his nose. He had a bad feeling about this one. Mind you, he often had a bad feeling about sudden and unexplained deaths; it sort of came with the territory. This was different. This felt a little too close to home.

He parked his Nissan on the verge and took a moment to assess the scene. The PC, keeping the public at bay, looked both bored and frozen. Beyond the tape, his sergeant, Geraint Drimple, was already berating some poor sod from forensics. He felt his groin itch and resisted the urge to scratch. Psychosomatic, he felt sure. 'Come on, Blane,' Pettimoron chided himself, 'this is a routine case.' Pettimoron pushed open the car door, knowing it would be anything but that.

He stood, shoulder to shoulder, with a DS Drimple and winced. "Those are his, I suppose."

Drimple nodded. "The SOCOs think they were excised pre-mortem. They don't know if they were used to suffocating him, though."

"Geez! Seriously? Why would someone do that?"

Drimple looked at his notes. "Seems the deceased - Dr Josiah Pretty - was a specialist in male infertility. Had a pretty good rep for curing all sorts of erectile dysfunction." He looked up. "Maybe a dissatisfied customer."

Pettimoron nodded and felt the itch return with a vengeance. He must not scratch.

The sergeant turned away and looked at the grand Tudor style building behind them.

"He practiced from here. Looks like whoever did this was waiting for him and attacked him before he could get indoors."

He looked up at the sound of voices. The Constable waved him over, and Drimple went and spoke to the woman with the PC. When he returned a few minutes later, Pettimoron had not moved, his gaze still held by the testicular gag. Drimple held a key aloft.

"Cleaner. Want a quick peek?"

"What about forensics?"

"The Prof is happy. Here," he offered blue plastic gloves and booties to his boss. He led the way. "According to Mrs. Pompous, or whatever her name was, he lived on the second floor. The first comprised his consulting rooms."

And the basement, thought Pettimoron, but kept that to himself.

As Drimple unlocked the door, he added, "We had a quick look around outside; no sign of a forced entry." He checked a slip of paper and entered a code, stilling the alarm. "Seems like the perp didn't break in. Where shall we start? His appointment book?"

"Probably on his computer." Pettimoron shuddered as he saw the blue door he remembered from before. "Try that."

If Drimple wondered why his boss had chosen that door, he did not question him, tugging it open. A light came on automatically. He disappeared inside; Pettimoron heard his sergeant as he descended the steps. He reappeared quickly. "It's pretty clinical. There are some other doors. Want to see what's there or do upstairs first?"

Pettimoron nodded to the basement. His sergeant stood back to let him go first.

The place was as he remembered: all white walls and tiles and sharp lighting.

Drimple moved past him and headed for the door at the far end of the room. Pettimoron waited. He was soon back. "I'm no expert, but it's a pretty neat operating theater. There's what I guess is a prep room and one with stores. All spotless." He turned through 360 degrees. "I guess it's legit."

Pettimoron pointed at a dark corner. He worked some saliva into his mouth and managed to ask, "What's over there?"

Drimple glanced where he pointed, narrowed his eyes, and headed across. "I wonder if... oh ho. Hang on." He smiled over his shoulder. "Your nose is working today, boss. You'd not know there was a door here unless you were right on top of it."

Pettimoron didn't move. He listened as Drimple worked on the door, scraping, telling him he'd got it open.

"Shall I?"

Pettimoron nodded, feeling sick. While Drimple disappeared into the gloom, hunting a switch, his mind flicked back ten weeks. At the time, it seemed like a consequence of the anaesthetic, the foggy image of the good doctor as he disappeared, apparently into the wall. Then he had been glad to get out, never liking anything medical, but that odd memory had stayed with him.

Drimple whistled softly as light poured out of the room. "Well, I'll be blowed."

As if a reluctant moth attracted to the light, Pettimoron slowly moved forward. He stopped on the room's threshold. Each wall was lined with small specimen jars, oddly old-fashioned amongst so much that was new. Even from where he stood, he could see each was neatly labelled with a spidery hand.

Drimple held up one jar to the light. "Good grief, they're balls. He kept people's balls." He looked at Pettimoron. "You okay, boss? You want a seat?"

Pettimoron stepped forward, shaking his head. He couldn't say why he wasn't surprised.

Drimple had begun to work his way down the shelving. "There must be hundreds. You think this is research, or he's just some sort of sicko?" He grinned at his boss. "Maybe the perp took umbrage and wanted his back." The DS moved along the second wall. "It's alphabetical." He took another jar. "These are enormous." He put them down. "The patients must have given permission, yes? He…" Drimple stopped, peering closely at a jar.

Pettimoron's heart stopped. The itch was beyond intolerable, and, despite himself, his hand reached down and scratched as Drimple turned to him, a curiously pitying expression on his face.

"This has your name on it, sir?" The sergeant's gaze dropped to where Pettimoron's hand had gone. "Or someone else with your name."

Pettimoron nodded. They both knew, given his name, that the chances of that were minuscule, about as likely as any man failing to notice he'd lost a testicle. "He didn't have permission, sergeant."

"Give us a motive, boss. And…"

Pettimoron looked up.

"I'll not say." He held out the jar. "Not a word."

Pettimoron held Drimple's gaze. They both knew that was a lie.

Discussion

HUGH: "I love open-ended stories where the reader can come to their own conclusion."

GEOFF: "One challenge in this case was Blane's interior monologue. How can I maintain the essential ambiguity in his position and not appear to be deliberately hiding anything from the reader (were there to be anything to hide)!? Is his nervousness a result of guilt or embarrassment? Glad it left you thinking (which was my aim), but is that as satisfying to you as a neat resolution?"

HUGH: "Where murder is involved, I think most readers like a resolution."

GEOFF: "When I wrote this, the main issue was the resolution. Should I point at the culprit? Or leave it to the reader to speculate? What is more satisfying? Are you shortchanged by this or given something for your imagination to work on after you've finished?"

CATHY: "I suppose it was about halfway through it became clear Pettimoron had been there before, and Something Was Up. I didn't get the impression he was necessarily the murderer – just one of a long list of possibilities. He knew the sergeant wouldn't keep the find to himself, but I reckoned he would spread the story all around the station to get a laugh. I got the impression his discomfort was from embarrassment rather than guilt

– otherwise, he would have been more concerned about getting into that basement and hiding the evidence."

ANNE: I never suspected for a moment that Pettimoron was the murderer – is that because embarrassment is more my thing?

Chapter Six:
"Miniature Planet"

BY DOUG JACQUIER

It was not the way that Geoffrey Owen Davies had envisaged his retirement working out. A career public servant, he'd not just survived but thrived with the arrival of technology and the privatisation of government services via the anodyne-sounding PPP (Public Private Partnerships). He made it to the finish line with his home paid for, a secure income from his superannuation for life, and some untraceable accounts in the Caymans. His wife had left some years ago and was now shacked up with a mutual colleague who apparently offered more excitement and a sense of adventure. That suited Geoffrey just fine.

Never a keen gardener in the past, growing had now become an obsession, albeit one with an emphasis on orderliness and strict boundaries. Over time, his wife's penchant for eclectic planting had turned much of their modestly sized garden into a jungle, a riot of randomness that offended his eye and troubled his soul. After she left, for the sake of not appearing to go senile, he retained some of the roses and the odd agapanthus, but the rest he unmercifully uprooted and replaced them with what he saw as useful raised beds of vegetables and fruit trees in large pots.

Of course, he could not eat even a small proportion of the seasonal harvests, so he gave most of it away to initially grateful (and then later inwardly groaning and discreetly binning) neighbours. Having used every square inch of arable land he owned (including what had previously been lawn), he had now taken advantage of the street gardening movement to colonise the verge in front of his home. He grew mostly herbs that he imagined passers-by would gratefully snip off to add to their evening meal. He even had a pair of scissors on a string hanging from a street tree. (Geoffrey had failed to observe that most of his neighbours still worked, rarely cooked, and never walked anywhere.)

When Mrs. Kafoops at No. 23 was taken into a nursing home, her grandson moved into her house, along with a few of his mates, allegedly with the brief to maintain the house and garden until such time as the house was sold. As vision-impaired Freddie could have predicted, that part of the contract was never met. The parties until dawn started, and most of Mrs. K's armchairs and couches ended up permanently residing on the increasingly weed-infested front and back lawns.

Geoffrey had never been comfortable with conflict, and, unlike his neighbours, he hadn't called the Police, and he had refused to sign a petition that was circulating, designed to have the lads removed.

However, there came a fateful day when a line was crossed, and Geoffrey would never be the same again. One morning, he was doing his rounds, inspecting his crops, when he stopped in his tracks. He stood gazing in horror at the carnage in his herb bed on the verge, clearly created by vehicles possessed by those attending the latest booze-and-drug-driven bacchanal at No. 23.

He walked briskly back inside and, as he sipped a cup of chamomile tea to calm his rarely disturbed nerves, he began to coldly map out his dish of revenge, followed by world domination (or at least that part of the world that comprised the street on which he lived).

Well aware that even the most meticulously planned strategies rarely survive the first exchange with the enemy, he allowed for some flexibility on the sequencing, but he knew that success depended on two key factors: contacts and anonymity. He congratulated himself on not having engaged in the mob rule tactics of his neighbours, including their futile attempts to seek firm Police action. That would potentially have left a trail to his door.

Crucial to his plan were his contacts within the building industry and local government. Mysterious deliveries of gravel and sand began appearing in the driveway of No.23, blocking their cars in (or out, as the case may be). The Council health inspector discovered an infestation of rats emanating from the premises. A 'routine' visit from the building inspector discovered termites were threatening the structural safety of the building. Police responded to an anonymous tip-off from union sources that the body of a victim of a factional dispute was buried in the backyard.

When Mrs. Kafoops' lawyer was contacted by the representative of a buyer (protected by commercial-in-confidence) with a halfway reasonable offer, they hastened to accept (while quietly wondering who this nutter could be). The grandson and his mates vanished from the scene.

Over the next few years, Geoffrey picked off his less desirable neighbours one by one. After the party boys came Cactus Man, with his front garden resembling the Mojave Desert and, shortly afterwards, the young people who believed the perfect garden involved red tanbark and gravel and a 'classic car' parked on it while it awaited restoration that never seemed to commence.

With each acquisition, he transformed its garden into the orderly and productive space it should always have been. His shelf-company corporation engaged agents to let the properties to people screened for their green fingers and their lack of desire to split asunder what God (or Geoffrey in this case) had put together. Any transgressions were met with instant eviction, encouraged by men with many tattoos and few teeth.

A decade from the commencement of his crusade, Geoffrey felt confident about claiming victory. He had created a miniature planet that was quiet, ordered, productive, and civilised. His street verge gardens fed and flavoured the surrounding streets, which had now become highly desirable moons orbiting around his world.

More than one PhD has been written about this phenomenon, and various theories have emerged as to how this had been achieved. Needless to say, none of them ventured down the path of speculating that this may have been the work of a benevolent dictator, drawing on the detritus of social democracy to create a new branch of social hygiene. Meanwhile, Geoffrey just smiled, confident that he would take his secrets to the grave and return to his plans for the neighbouring streets.

Discussion

GEOFF: "Geoffrey has an intriguing back story. His Cayman Island accounts, his access to and his use of 'encouragers' to get his way leaves me wondering who this 'gray man' really is. A career public servant could be a contract killer for the secret services with a little sideline in assassination funding his sociopathic retirement. Because I have these questions, I've ended up feeling a little short changed. Is he some sort of horticultural Walter White driven to excess by the callous obliteration of his beloved tarragon? Will Geoffrey succeed in creating Stepford for vegans? Part of me hopes so... well done, Doug."

HUGH: "This story reminded me of an episode of The X-Files where Mulder and Scully investigated horrible goings-on in a neighbourhood where even one blade of grass was out of place, got something horrible happening to the house owner of the garden said blade of grass was. Even a flickering streetlight outside a house was seen as not acceptable. I can't remember the episode's outcome, other than some kind of monster coming out of the floor at night to take away the resident who had not fixed the fault. Maybe Geoffrey is that monster from the X-files that has been able to transform itself into a human? You mentioned 'The Twilight Zone' Marsha. There was an episode that featured the perfect street where the residents all turned on each other. I won't give away the twist, but Rod Serling said it was one of his favourite episodes."

CATHY: "The initials of Mr G O Davies are interesting. Is this the author's general impression of career public servants or just this particular one? I have to say that as a career public servant myself (in libraries), I came away with my local government pension after forty years but, sadly, no Cayman Islands accounts. Nonetheless, with the advent of the party animals, I felt quite sorry for colourless, imaginative Geoffrey, content to bring order to his home surroundings with no ambition to upscale – although I did wonder what he planned to do with all that money."

ANNE: "Have to say I have a LOT of sympathy for Geoffrey. Noise from neighbours drives me nuts, and I have fantasies of forcing everyone to do it MY way! I think it's always the case that when we try to create the perfect system, it backfires. We need that variety even when we hate it."

Chapter Seven: "Nailing It"

BY ANNE STORMONT

"Stop it," Evie begged. She looked at the pile of dirty dishes – her mother's best china. Mother had insisted that everyone should come back to the house for tea and insisted on the good cups and saucers.

"Should have done them last night," her mother repeated. "I said, didn't I? But, oh no, too lazy for that––or too drunk."

"Drunk?" Evie said. "You know I don't drink."

"Oh, really? I wasn't cold in my grave yesterday, and you were at it."

"One whisky, Mother, at your wake – to warm me up. It was bloody freezing at the cemetery."

"Swearinganddrinking.Noself-control,justlikeyourfather."

'*Here we go,*' Evie thought. She knew nothing could stop her mother – not even being dead.

Her mother's voice continued. "No wonder Derek left you. Typical of you, messing up a good marriage to a decent, respectable man."

"I *left* him, Mother, because he *hit* me – the Reverend Derek hit me."

"I never saw any marks."

"I hid them – I hid them from everybody."

"You probably drove him to it with your simpering ways. He was a good, god-fearing man. He wouldn't have meant to hurt you."

"He put me in hospital!"

Evie could hear her mother tut, could see her vinegary pout.

"He took you on when no other man would. You, with your wanton ways. You always did need a tight rein – even then, you strayed."

A bleak laugh mixed with the bile in Evie's throat.

"It was no laughing matter," her mother said. "It was sinful, disgraceful."

"I was eighteen. I was in love. I––"

"You were eighteen and pregnant. Disgusting little slut."

Evie imagined the stiff, clawed hands reaching out of the coffin and felt her mother's grip on her wrist. She recoiled, breathed against the nausea, and tried to slam the lid down – but her mother was still too strong for her.

"It's just as well your father was already dead. The embarrassment would have killed him."

Evie thought of her beloved father and saw his lovely smile as he scooped her up and sat her on his red motorcycle. He'd died thirty years ago when she was ten – left the house one day and never came back. Eva felt suddenly bold. "You killed Daddy. Broke him with your cruel words."

Her mother didn't answer.

"And you killed my baby."

Evie dared to think she'd silenced her mother's ghost.

But then, the voice returned, "It wasn't a baby. It was a shameful liability. I arranged to have it dealt with quickly and discreetly."

"Shut up!" Evie slammed her hands down on the worktop. One arm curled around the unwashed crockery and swept it onto the stone floor. "Leave me alone!"

Evie gasped, drenched with the shock of unfamiliar emotions – rage, passion, and joy – the sheer unrestrained joy of being alive. The coffin lid had closed.

Evie's father had ensured that the house would pass to Evie on her mother's death. The dark Victorian villa in Edinburgh reeked of her mother, and selling it felt like the first nail in her mother's coffin.

The local church was the sole beneficiary of her mother's money. When the minister called to thank her, she told Evie that the money would be split between the local women's refuge and a church support programme for teenage mothers. "Well, that's two more nails in the bitch's coffin," Evie had said, laughing.

A few weeks later, on a sunny Saturday morning in Inverness, she was on her way home from a walk in her local park. It was then that she saw it. It glinted in the sunshine as if it was winking at her. She crossed the forecourt of the motorcycle dealership to have a closer look. It was sleek and red with chrome trims. She ran her hand along its seat, caught the scent of leather and oil, and squeezed the grips on the handlebars.

"Beautiful, isn't she?"

Evie looked around. A man stood beside her. He looked about Evie's age and was dressed in overalls. He extended his hand. "Ted," he said. "Ted Roberts, owner of this establishment."

"Evie," she replied, shaking his hand. "Yes, she *is* beautiful, and I'd like to buy her."

Ted smiled, and Evie noticed that it was a lovely, warm, open smile. "Right," he said. "Well, that's the easiest sale I've ever made! Come inside, and we'll do the paperwork."

"Do you want it delivered, or will you come and collect it?" Ted asked when they'd concluded the deal.

"I'll need it delivered. I don't have a licence – yet."

"Okay," said Ted, smiling again. "No problem."

Evie thought about how she liked his smile, liked how Ted appeared neither mocking nor judgemental.

"Or I could keep it here – until you're ready to drive it away yourself."

"Oh, no, I couldn't ask you to do that."

"Please, I want to. You can visit the bike whenever you like. Actually, I hope you will – that way, I know I'll see you again."

Evie laughed. "Okay, then I'll leave it here."

"Happy?" Ted asked, slipping his arm around Evie and smiling his gorgeous smile.

"Oh, yes," she replied, kissing him on the mouth.

It was a year to the day since they'd met. It was wet and windy, and they had the top deck of the cross-channel ferry to themselves. Their motorbikes were stowed below. They planned to spend their honeymoon biking down through France and Spain.

Ted took her in his arms, pushed her windswept hair back from her face, and kissed her long and slowly.

"I'm so glad we decided to do this," Evie said a little while later, still standing in her husband's embrace. "It'll be so lovely just taking our time, doing whatever we fancy..."

"And what might you fancy?" Ted grinned.

"You, Mr Roberts – you," Evie said, smiling back.

Ted laughed. "You're a wanton hussy. Do you know that?"

"Yes, I am. I am!" Evie raised her arms in the air. "Wanton and proud of it!" she called to the gulls circling overhead. Ted laughed again. Evie looked at him. She'd never felt so happy.

And that was the final nail in her mother's coffin.

Discussion

CATHY: "I could see and hear Evie's controlling mother... until I read that she wasn't actually present. Still, Evie was under her influence, reaching out from the grave to continue her domination. It was good to follow Evie's recovery, from the first thought of rebellion prompted by her lost father to the act of rebellion that closes the coffin. We enjoy hearing of the nails that keep it down – the spiteful disinheriting of her daughter, which is turned against her wishes – and the new life that buries the old witch for good. I particularly liked that the final nail in her mother's coffin was to revel in the freedom to be wanton – the term originally hurled by her mother as a condemnation."

HUGH: "As soon as I knew that Evie's mother was dead, and that she was hearing her voice in her head, mental health problems came to mind. It's probably because I recently listened to a radio show about people who hear voices in their heads and how it's often connected to mental health. It makes me wonder if Ted is indeed a lucky man to have married Evie. And (according to her mother's voice) hadn't she strayed from a marriage once before? Whilst I condemn violence of any kind, is that why Reverend Derek had hit her when he found out that Evie had been unfaithful? I still feel rather sorry for Ted."

GEOFF: "Well, let's think about that. We are given Evie's take, her representation of her mother. Is that self-serving rather than accurate...sure Mother might be overprotective, and Evie increasingly resented that monster, which would justify her antagonism. Mother is dead – how? Evie the poisoner? Now, being hit isn't ever justified, nor is it taking away a child – was the child adopted or killed? Another ambiguity. Hugh's mental health theory might have merit."

ANNE S: "Interesting debate! Even I don't know all the answers. I hadn't even thought of the questions! I didn't mean to suggest Evie had been unfaithful – simply that she followed (or tried to) follow her own path, which wasn't the one approved by her mother. As for the 'simpering' that was the mother/husband's way of describing Evie, expressing an opinion. I see Evie as standing up for herself rather than beating herself up. She's replaying old conversations in her head – not because of any sort of mental illness as in 'hearing voices' but as a way of reflecting and having her say."

DOUG: "Short stories need to stand on their own two feet, with us as readers accepting what we've been given on their own terms. To me, it's a story of a determined young woman, deserted by her loving father, abused by her husband, and verbally tortured by a harridan mother, but finding a way to desert them all in return. Well done on a great story that has got us all talking and debating. That's exactly what **'Story Chat'** is all about."

GARY: "I loved the final jolt you gave us, or at least me. In your final scene, Ted calls her a "wanton hussy." I thought for sure Evie would not be able to take this remark as Ted intended, but as a painful fresh injury taken right from the script of her mother's love-less abuse. Her response, instead of exploding the relationship, became a huge piece of evidence of her escaping the battle scene between her and her ghost of a mom. You dropped me into a state of "Oh-no!" but instead let Evie step up and crush the unintended insult."

Chapter Eight:
"The Apple Doesn't Fall
Far from the Tree"

BY DEBBIE HARRIS

It felt like *yesterday* in her heart, but in her head, she knew it was almost fifty years ago.

The day when everything she knew about life had irrevocably changed – the fateful stormy day she'd become a new *mother*.

It was a day in late May, with winter setting in. The days were gray and wet, but every now and again, a bright, clear, sunny day was a welcome relief and brightened the whole world. Unfortunately, it hadn't been one of those bright, clear days when it all happened. Instead, a storm was raging, roiling, thundering, lighting the sky with shards of electricity. Was it an omen? She often wondered about that.

Becoming a mother hadn't been high on her bucket list. In fact, she'd been *sitting on the fence* about the whole motherhood thing, but the pressure from the state officials, family, especially her husband, and her friends had been mounting for the past few years. They'd been married for 4 years already, and people were starting to ask questions, quite probing personal questions in fact – when would they be starting their family, were they trying, did they have fertility issues, were they scared?

Really, it was no one else's business at all – except it was.

The rules stated, 'after 5 years of marriage, a baby must have been initiated by the couple. Otherwise, medical intervention would be implemented,' – such official, impersonal language. Typical of the state!

She'd known she was pregnant the minute it happened, and she was happy when it was confirmed by the medical team assigned to her. Her only problem throughout the whole nine months was her inability to eat *apples* in any way, shape or form – apple pie, apple sauce, apple cake, apple juice – apparently, she was one in a million that had this reaction. She was watched carefully as the apple symptoms were considered a throwback to earlier times and were the harbinger of some darkness.

When she finally started feeling the contractions and knew her baby had started on its journey, she and her husband battled the storm to get to the hospital in time.

The labour went well, and she delivered a beautiful, healthy baby girl. She and her husband felt ecstatic. They kissed the baby girl, checked out all her fingers and toes, and congratulated themselves on their cleverness. They were now a 'proper' family.

The baby was whisked away after a few minutes, and when she questioned this, she was painstakingly ignored by all the medical staff.

Everything was rosy until it wasn't.

She never saw her baby girl again. She was told all sorts of things – reasons why her baby wasn't able to be returned to her, things were said about her baby's condition that didn't make sense to her, and they were encouraged to try again for another baby.

It was a fateful day indeed, but here she was fifty years later, ready to meet a strange woman who had contacted her through the underground network. She was told it was highly secretive, and so she hadn't told a soul of the meeting. Her husband had passed away from a broken heart many years ago, and it was just her these days.

She was anticipating some good news, but it was a massive shock to her system when the woman walked in, smiling eyes dancing, her bright red curly hair lighting up the room. It was like looking in a mirror.

That old saying, the apple doesn't fall far from the tree, flashed through her mind and was never truer than in this instance!

Discussion

SUZANNE: "Wow, this story was so unexpected and creepy but SO well written, and I want to read more now! Well done. I sort of want to know more about that crazy society, why couples HAVE to have babies, why the baby is taken away... and much more."

DENYSE: "That is so NOT like I expect from my blogging friend, Deb! But, of course, she has been spreading her writing songs and delving into that deep & mysterious field called FICTION."

GARY: "You did not give your protagonist a name. This was a surprise. Were you suggesting that in this **slightly off-world** she lives in, her name is not important? Brilliant! This felt so wrong, and I bet it will outrage some readers, but you left us knowing that her husband was broken-hearted, but was she? You did a neat thing by taking "being a mom" off of her bucket list, but still — that should have cratered her soul. Another sign of this world? Perhaps it was somehow common for babies to be taken...Ugh!"

JANIS: "I would have loved to know more about the horrible circumstances behind that poor (unnamed) woman having her child taken from her. Was it unique to her, or did others have their newborns taken away, too...? If so, how did she not hear about it before giving birth? What did her aversion to apples mean? I think you've written a terrific story that you could flush out and make into a longer one (even a novel).

CATHY: "I never met my birth mother, although I was able to apply for my original birth certificate in the 1960s when the adoption law changed in the UK. I didn't take it further, not wanting to turn up on the doorstep of someone who had very effectively hidden my existence. (Apparently, she was a twin whose sister covered for her while she was having me.) Also, my adoptive parents were giving each other grief, so I didn't want to be saddled with another needy parent. Re the story, I suspect there may be a hint there in the 'throwback' reference, which kind of justifies mention of the apple antipathy."

Chapter Nine:
Sometimes a Miracle

BY GARY A. WILSON

In the summer of 1961, Rockford was twenty-four and could not have been prepared the afternoon his wife tried to reach him at a job site.

The homeowner hurried out to tell him, "Rock, Carolyn just called. She needs you to meet them at the hospital. Something's wrong with Ann."

He asked, "Did she say what? Ann had a sore throat the past few days, but…"

"Ann's fever went higher. She called the doctor, who told her to hurry to the hospital. Rock, she's really scared. Go — please go."

"Thanks, Martha. I'll call when…"

"Shoo! Just go."

Rockford and Carolyn Jensen had married right after graduating from high school. They both worked after school, dated, then married, and quickly started their new lives together. Carolyn dreamed of college, but children happened instead. Rock struggled with academics, so he never considered college because he could build or fix almost anything. Even with his job at the tile store, Rock was always working side jobs to earn extra money for the family. On this day, their son, Arthur, was five, and Ann was only three. Rock began to fear as he climbed into his truck. What could be wrong with Ann that we have to rush to the hospital?

When he arrived, Rock was directed to a waiting room where Carolyn and Arthur were sitting. As soon as she saw him, she hurried to the reception desk and told the nurse that her husband had arrived. She ran over to him and into his arms.

"Babe, something terrible is happening. Her fever got so high, and they took her from me and wouldn't let us go with her. The doctor wanted you to be here to tell us both what's happening."

The doctor appeared and came to sit with them.

"Hello Rock. I'm sorry to drag you in, but I need to tell you that Ann is very sick. There are two common bacterial infections. They're named staphylococcus and streptococcus, and they're both serious. You'll hear them abbreviated 'staph' and 'strep.' The test cultures aren't back from the lab yet, but we are certain that Ann has had both for several days."

At this, Carolyn gasped and uttered, "Her sore throat and... and those blisters on her face..."

"Yes, strep presents a burning sore throat and turns into rheumatic fever, which causes heart damage. Staph is giving her those blisters. It can follow her blood system to damage her lungs or heart or lots of other organs. Her symptoms are getting worse fast."

Rock was stunned, almost unable to imagine his child being so sick.

Carolyn visibly struggled to remain calm, but asked, "What can you do?"

"We've isolated her to prevent spreading either disease, so she's scared. And we've started her on sulfa antibiotics that fight both strep and staph, but they don't work as well as they used to. This is why I wanted to talk to you both. You need to understand that Ann's infections are fully developed, and if the sulfa meds don't work, we don't have anything else to try."

"Rock, Carolyn, I'm sorry, but we could lose her in just a few days."

Rock was overwhelmed.

Carolyn struggled to contain her tears, but failed as Rock took her in his arms.

"Nurse, please watch Arthur while I take them to their daughter."

Past some double doors, their long walk through the hospital, antiseptic smells, the echoing sounds, and the bright florescent lights together transformed that hallway into the longest, darkest path any parent could travel.

Rock held Carolyn close as they looked through the window into the isolation ward. Ann was laid out with tubes and machines attached to her tiny body. Her face was now half covered with open, puffy blisters. This was their baby Ann in the middle of a living nightmare.

"One of you can gown up and go see her." Carolyn insisted on going, so the doctor took Rock back to the waiting room.

Over the next two days, they sent Arthur to stay with family while they tried different sulfa drugs, and Ann only got worse.

In tears one afternoon, Carolyn reported through the glass window, "Rock, she's choking on the pain in her throat. She's lost her voice, and those damned sulfa drugs are worthless!"

Rock and Carolyn's souls were shredding as they helplessly watched Ann's face disappear behind a grotesque mask of festering blisters, and her moving only to spasm through a stabbing cough followed by her weak cries of pain.

One afternoon, their exhausted doctor was trying to give them the latest bad news about how they were going to try even stronger sulfa drugs that might have harmful side effects. Carolyn was almost empty of tears, and Rock was barely able to think when an administrator rushed into the room and approached the doctor.

"Sorry to interrupt, but Doctor, you wanted to know immediately when we have any response from the pharmacy supplier. They called and left this message."

The doctor snatched the paper and smiled as he read.

"Rock, Carolyn, this might be the news we've been praying for. There's a new antibiotic that has just become available. It's not another sulfa drug and has been known for years, but production has been limited, but now we have it. Tomorrow, we'll be starting Ann on a new drug with a startling record of success. Finally, this — is very good news."

"What is it?" Rock asked.

"You may have heard of penicillin. The newest version is ampicillin and is being called a miracle drug."

Within two weeks after starting on ampicillin, Ann was home and playing with friends as normal.

This fictional story was based on actual events. In the real account, my younger sister was miraculously saved by this just-in-time new drug. Ampicillin was our miracle drug in 1961. Within two weeks after starting on ampicillin, she was home and playing with friends as normal and 60 years later, she's enjoying a normal life.

Discussion

JANIS: "That would have been such a frightening situation! Gary, you did a great job grabbing and maintaining my interest and making the reader feel the tension and stress the parents found themselves in. As someone who is allergic to sulfa-based drugs, I am doubly pleased that better alternatives have been developed. As Sue mentioned, we are running out of options, especially with the over/misuse of antibiotics. No parent should have to go through what Ann's (and, I guess, your parents, Gary) went through."

YVETTE: "You kept this short and masterfully succinct – felt the action, and it is a great reminder of the power of medicine. I had a professor in the early 1990s – Dr. Beal – who was an emeritus – and was retired and at our school teaching Botany for fun – he was an entomologist and a cool guy. Anyhow, he said he briefly worked (in the late 40s) with folks who worked on penicillin in the late 20s (something like that) – he had some connection and was proud of it. I am also glad that antibiotics are not being overprescribed as I think there have been decades where that happened – and in my very humble opinion – I have seen so many folks sick with autoimmune disorders who also have had antibiotics "too many times to count" – is there a correlation?"

Doug: "As a childhood polio survivor myself, I have every reason to thank the dedicated medical scientists who found the vaccine that I missed by a few years. I'd encourage everyone to read more about the discovery and development of penicillin, including the fact that Howard Florey from my home State of South Australia shared the Nobel Prize with Fleming and others. It was Florey, along with Ernst Chain, who actually made a useful and effective drug out of penicillin after the task had been abandoned as too difficult by its discoverer, Fleming."

Leslie: "I held my breath all the way through this story. As a child, my mother had scarlet fever as a result of a similar infection and had to learn to walk again. The family was quarantined, and my grandfather was unable to work. It was a very difficult time. But Mom has lived to be 94 years old and is still doing well. Penicillin was definitely a miracle drug for so many. I was given it so many times I have developed a life-threatening allergic reaction to it. But have also outgrown many of the infections I had as a child. Great story, Gary."

Hugh: "They say the best stories are based on true stories. This one is one of those stories. I'm not a fan of medical dramas, but I was hooked by your story, Gary. I liked it as well because you gave me a glimpse into the introduction of penicillin. Most of us have heard of it, but probably don't know someone who was at the forefront of it being used to save lives so early on."

Gary: "There are several ways to tell history, and I've always liked the approach of historical fiction. I created characters similar to my family, but scrambled things to make it fiction and more focused than our real account of events. But I liked the idea of taking readers to a difficult place at a time when they did not have the benefit of the technologies we have today, giving them a terrible situation, even a hopeless one, and trying to capture what they must have felt. The image of a child dying for lack of a solution we have readily in hand has been a powerful one for me because it is a real memory."

Chapter Ten:
"Dress for a Princess"

BY WENDY FLETCHER

I am hot and tired, and I know that I shouldn't have put off this trip to the shops until the last minute, but that seems to have become my style in the past few months. Shopping with a toddler is testing reserves I didn't know I had, and I fear that they will run out at any moment.

The assistants had smiled and been polite, but I am left with the impression they would have preferred us to shop elsewhere. We have asked for more than they can offer, and they have done their best to accommodate us, but it is an uneasy compromise.

Pushing these thoughts out of the way to deal with later, I turn back to Alicia. She is excited about this afternoon's party and giggles as I try awkwardly to zip her into a frothy pink dress.

I try to stay calm and not dampen her enthusiasm, but I am struggling. It has been another long day in an unbelievably long year.

She is almost three now, and every day brings more exciting discoveries for her and more unforeseen challenges for me. We had fought through sleepless nights when her screams reached neighbouring houses, and in the morning found us huddled under a duvet, too exhausted to face the day. We have travelled together on the precarious road of frustration that leads to potty training. This term, she has started nursery school and made her first friends outside the family. I have watched her grow more independent, and my heart has been torn. Part of me is delighted that she is developing into a relatively normal child. Part of me wants to keep her safely cocooned against my shoulder, the unknowing baby who won't have to field awkward questions and face the cruel realities of life.

It was at nursery that she met the new little friend who had invited her to the birthday party this afternoon, and my thoughts returned to the dress. The length is about right, but she still has that chubby layer of baby fat on her torso, and the stitching pulls tight across the chest. I try to stop her from bouncing long enough to check the label to make sure it corresponds with the ticket on the coat hanger. It does, but I am still not convinced. 'Age two to three' sounds quite vague now. Does this mean that all children of two and three conform to this standard?

Evidently not. Mine is definitely stretching the boundaries. I thought we were coming out of the phase where she pushed away all my culinary efforts, despite much persuasion. Now I wonder if I have been over-feeding her. Is she already on the slippery slope to a bad diet?

Another problem to examine later, but right now, I have to deal with the reality that I have picked the wrong size for my child. She is almost three, so perhaps it is time to look at 'Age three to four.' Such a silly, trivial mistake, but I am cross with myself. It means that I have to get her out of the dress again and clothed in her own little skirt and jumper, complete with tights and boots.

Whoever invented lace-up boots for toddlers?

Then we will have to trail back across the shop floor to the rail and only hope that it comes in a bigger size. If I could properly explain this to her, it would be easier, but her vocabulary is limited. At this moment, it is limited to 'Princess, 'licia be princess.'

I cannot make her understand that we will get another dress, the same but bigger – hopefully. She resists in the only way she knows – by making the removal of the garment as difficult as possible. She wriggles and protests as she is buttoned back into her own clothes, pushing away my hands and wrapping determined little fingers around my wrists. I know the thought she cannot express is that the beautiful pink dress with its shimmering decorations is about to disappear from her life. She is disappointed, and I hate to see disappointment in her soft hazel eyes, now clouded with tears.

The most hurtful part is that it's not about the dress. It's about me. She is disappointed that I have offered her something and then taken it away again. She is even more disappointed that I have not heeded her pleas, and for just a moment, I am tempted to put the dress back on her and let her walk proudly out of the shop, but I know I mustn't.

I must find a way of coping with the emotions I see in her eyes. I will see more disappointment. I will see hurt and pain and anguish. I have to learn to deal with those looks of confusion, bewilderment, and a sense of injustice. I have to mop up the stream of tears that gush forth and hold back my own until the day comes when we might cry together and mourn the loss of her mother.

Only then – maybe – will we be able to find some humour in our lives again and perhaps even laugh about the day we went shopping to buy her first party dress and had to clamber into a tiny, unlit storage area beyond a mountain of boxes that were waiting to be unpacked because there were changing rooms for ladies and girls, and changing rooms for men and boys but we didn't fit into their perceived vision of a family. We were just a lost little girl, and a bereaved Dad, trying to find our way to some kind of normality.

Discussion

Because this post appeared on a guest host's blog, I didn't have access to the comments. The host had computer problems, which ate that post, and anyone who has worked on a computer can relate to the fact they sometimes do things on their own!

Chapter Eleven:
Puddles

BY HUGH W. ROBERTS

I wanted to be like my daddy and be a lifesaver until I heard Mummy say that he'd made her life a misery.

Mummy said that Daddy was horrible to her. But I never understood how he could be nasty and be a lifesaver.

Aren't lifesavers meant to be nice?

Daddy has always been kind to my friends, but not to me. But he never saved Mummy's life. Do you know that she left home one night when I was fast asleep? I woke up, and she was gone. The nice police lady asked me some questions while others helped Daddy look for Mummy, but they never found her.

Now I have a new mummy.

I don't like her very much, though.

She's the one who brings parcels to us and who I saw in Mummy and Daddy's bedroom with Daddy before Mummy left. Daddy told me not to tell anyone, not even you! Please don't tell him I've told you; otherwise, he may do nasty things to us.

My friends Teddy and Giraffe told me not to trust Daddy or my new mummy. Do you like Teddy and Giraffes? They're my best friends and always tell me the truth.

One day, I decided I wanted to be like Daddy. Not nasty, but to save lives. I rescued Teddy and Giraffe from a big puddle at the top of the cliff. It was left by a strange storm that Daddy said Mummy had sent to come and get me. He really scared me when he said that to me. I started to cry. Teddy and Giraffe were not pleased with him. They told me to tell Daddy that I had just saved them from the puddle.

I know; I saw you save them from falling in. It's a strange puddle that Mummy's weird storm left, isn't it? Why don't we go home and play our secret game again before your new mummy gets home?

But I didn't want to play the secret game with Daddy because I don't like playing it. I want to play with Teddy and Giraffe, not play Daddy's secret game.

Aren't you a bit old for Teddy and Giraffe? Daddy asked. You're 8 years old tomorrow and shouldn't be playing with soft toys anymore.

NO! I shouted back. My real mummy said Teddy and Giraffe are my best friends, and they'll look after me. They tell me everything. I do whatever they tell me, and they said no special games today with Daddy.

Daddy was very angry when I shouted at him. He tried taking Teddy and Giraffe off me, but I bit him on the arm to make him stop.

YOUR REAL MUMMY? he shouted at me. YOU HAVEN'T SEEN YOUR REAL MUMMY FOR MONTHS, AND YOU NEVER WILL!

YES, I DID, I shouted back. I SAW MUMMY IN THE STRANGE PUDDLE YOU SAID SHE SENT TO GET ME. She's in there. Go look, Daddy.

At first, Daddy didn't believe me, but he eventually went over and looked in the puddle.

There's nothing in there. You're seeing things, you silly girl. Now, come home with me and let's play our special game, he said angrily.

NO! SHE'S THERE! Look closer, Daddy. Mummy, show Daddy you're there.

That's when Teddy and Giraffe told me what to do next.

Thank you for saving our lives, they whispered. Now push your nasty daddy into the puddle. We're here to save you.

While Daddy continued to investigate the puddle, I put Teddy and Giraffe down, went behind him, pushed him hard, and waited for the splash. But there wasn't one. The only thing I saw when I looked was Daddy's face looking up at me from the puddle. I thought I heard him calling for help, but Teddy and Giraffe said to go home and call the nice police lady.

They told me to tell her what Daddy was doing to me.

I tried calling the nice police lady on my toy phone, but she wouldn't answer. The only person that speaks to me on my phone is my real mummy. I love it when my phone rings, and it's my real mummy.

My new mummy will be home soon. I don't like her. Did I tell you that I saw her in Mummy's and Daddy's bedroom?

Would you like to play the secret game Daddy and I play? I know I said I didn't like it much, but it's got a funny name... Snakes and Ladders. That's a funny name for a game, isn't it? Snakes can't climb ladders, can they?

We're not allowed to play it when my other mummy is home, so we'll have to play it quickly. Did I tell you that she's scared of snakes? I heard her say she'd die of shock if she saw a snake. That's funny, isn't it?

Oh, look. It's raining again. Do you think my real mummy will send any more puddles and send Daddy back? I hope not, but maybe just one more puddle that I can push my new mummy into.

Discussion

KIRSTIN: "creepy but intriguing story,"

CINDY: "I think it would be a great story for therapists and kids that have been abused."

CATHY: "When she tells of Mummy calling her on her toy phone, the disturbed child becomes more disturbing."

TERRI: "Hugh writes some twisted tales."

GEOFF: "I think we need to assume some supernatural element as well as an unreliable narrator."

NORAH: "That little girl seems very evil while covering her maliciousness with seeming innocence."

KL: "I was wondering if there was something malevolent about the toys or some form of split personality in which the toys were displaying one side of her and her story another."

JT: "Combining horror with humor is really your "bag," Hugh."

DEBBIE: "I felt a real Twilight Zone vibe and wondered about that 'magic' puddle. I also appreciate that the mother may have had issues, and the daughter is very insightful in her thoughts."

GLORIA: "I think the new mummy needs to watch her back!"

Chapter Twelve:
"Broaching the Subject"

BY DOUG JACQUIER

We were sorting through Mum's personal possessions before she moved into the aged-care facility, and we'd come to her ornate Japanese jewellery box. She carefully sorted the contents into two groups: one to take with her (and leave to me when she passed) and one for her favorite charity shop. In her personal pile, I noticed a cheap costume jewellery red brooch, which I thought was seriously at odds with her usual good taste.

Picking it up, I said, 'Sentimental value?'

'You could say that,' she replied, with a slight tilt of her head and a movement at the corner of her mouth. I was prepared to leave it at that, assuming it was a memory she'd rather keep to herself, but then she began to breathe very shallowly, and her already wafery skin turned to a shade of alabaster.

Deeply concerned, I said quickly, 'Mum, are you OK? Do you want me to call the doctor? Can you speak?'

She seemed to have returned from somewhere else, and her colour improved a little.

'Sit down. There's something I want to tell you that you must promise me you will never share.'

'Of course, Mum.'

'I mean it, and you will understand when I tell you.'

I sat next to her, my mind shuffling through a myriad of possibilities: a secret affair, a love child, a theft…

She began timorously, but her voice gained strength as her tale unfolded.

'During the war, life changed a great deal for women. Out of necessity, we took up trades, ran farms, drove heavy vehicles, and all the other things that men had kept to themselves. We were even shown how to use guns, just in case the enemy ever invaded.'

Somehow, this wasn't gelling with the bird-like, frail person in front of me and the home-body mother I thought I knew, but I didn't interrupt.

'When the war ended, and the lucky men came home to their families, they took all those jobs back, and the so-called natural order of things gradually returned. But many of those men, especially the ones who'd spent time in POW camps, had changed in ways we could never have imagined were possible.'

Here, she paused and began gnawing at her bottom lip. Again concerned, I leaned forward to comfort her, but she gestured me away.

'Let me finish.'

In control again, she continued, gathering momentum with each sentence.

'Some just sat in silence, some just sat and cried, some couldn't hold down a job, some became drunks, some became gamblers, and some became wife-beaters. There was no help for them or their families beyond pulling up their bootstraps and getting on with it. Frightened, destitute families were in every town and suburb, and there was no welfare safety net then. And so, it began.'

For goodness' sake, Mum, what began my mind was screaming, but I said nothing.

'Nobody knows, or has told, who started it, but I remember at women's gatherings and down at the shops back then, a small number of women were wearing the same tacky red brooch you see here. Over a cuppa one day, I asked a very close friend if she had noticed it, too. She had, she said, and she knew what it meant. It meant that the woman knew of a case.'

Impatient, I said, 'What sort of case?'

'A case of a man who could not be put back together again. A man whose friends and family had done all they could to bring him back to the human race but failed. A man who had beaten, raped, gambled, or drank to the point that the misery he was inflicting was no longer tolerable, but society seemed unwilling or uninterested in stopping him.'

I blinked involuntarily and rapidly and said, 'So what happened to these cases?'

'They were removed.'

'What do you mean removed?'

'Someone in the network with no other connections would remove him. A drunk might go to sleep on a railway track. A gambler might be found floating in the river, and rumors spread of unpaid debts to criminals. A rapist might accidentally fall into a machine at work. A man's gun might accidentally go off while he was cleaning it. There were ways.'

I could no longer hide my shock. 'But Mum, that's vigilante stuff! What if you got it wrong?'

'Oh, we were never wrong. If a woman reported a case, it would be thoroughly investigated by others before the removal was undertaken. That was part of the point of the network.'

'But didn't the police get suspicious about all these deaths?'

'Oh, you make it sound like some sort of bloodbath. It's not as if there were hundreds. Besides, there were police in critical positions to whom we could have a quiet word about not getting too enthusiastic about investigating further.'

'So, there were men in the network as well?'

'Not in the network as such, but, yes, there were men who were prepared to be helpful should the need arise. They'd also learned some new skills during the war.'

'Is it still going?'

'Don't have a clue, really, but I haven't seen that red brooch in public for donkey's years. But I thought I'd put it in your pile in case it might be useful in the future. I mean, I heard about some of these men returning from the Middle East...,' and she trailed off.

The only thing I could think of was to change the subject, so I shifted to my father, who had died not long after I was born. I asked whether there were any of his things that she would like to take with her.

'Oh, no, dear, I got rid of those a long time ago. I truly loved him when I married him, but he was never the same after the war.'

The briefest of pauses, and then she said brightly, 'How about a nice cup of tea?'

Discussion

JANIS: "I love this story! So well-written and engaging. Even though the "reveal" wasn't too surprising (after all, she had one of the brochures), the way it was written led the reader so satisfyingly to the conclusion. Well done... I hope to read more stories from you.

GARY: "I also love that a story told in first person opens the door to an imperfect, non-omniscient or even dishonest storyteller, all stuff an omniscient narrator can't get away with. So this story really pulled me in, and I felt very much like Mum wanted to get this history off her chest and have someone she knows and trusts to carry it further... "Oh, we were never wrong." was strikingly audacious. Really? I liked how Mum mentioned that the investigators were uninvolved with the "case" themselves, but still – wow! ... The likely ending was easy to guess earlier and still was a very satisfying wrap-up to a great story. Bravo Doug"

DONNA: "This was fantastic! Could certainly be true, and I do believe I will keep my eye out for a brooch. Wink. But in the real world, thank goodness we understand more about PTSD (Post Traumatic Stress Disorder), and it is possible for them to get help. I think the mother would have felt pretty relieved as a chance to come clean with what she felt was right... and wrong. Wow! Captive audience here."

YVETTE: "I am so glad that I read this historical fiction based on a true story. Jacquier really lets us feel the body changes and emotions with the grandmother and shares the secret connecting to the brooch. It reminded me that the aftermath of war is long-reaching, and I hope those coming back from recent wars get the help they need. Enjoyed this story very much.”

D.: “Great story, Doug. I thought it was pretty clear that she was sharing the story to pass on the idea and the possible help from the network should it be necessary to the narrator. Wars continue, and domestic issues due to war damage continue. And the hint of how Dad died... nicely done. The brooch is truly a family heirloom. The narrator has been inducted into the network and given a bit of family history.”

Chapter Thirteen: "On the Streets"

BY CATHY CADE

Lights twinkled around decorated market stalls, and angels swung overhead. The usual wafts of burger onions and hot doughnuts mingled with hints of cinnamon and mulled wine spices.

Outside Starbucks, a guitar busker belted out *Rudolph the Red-nosed Reindeer* while a small group of children laughed at the faces she pulled around her red plastic nose. Matt wished he'd thought of that. He had red noses from Red Nose days at school squirrelled away in his bedroom drawer.

It was freezing! If Mum hadn't suggested he leave his busking for a warmer day, he might have put this off. There would be less competition after Christmas. She'd said it was too soon to go out on the streets after coming back from university with a head cold. He'd told her he didn't need her permission.

Ahead was a singer whose backing came from a boombox; how far did the volume from that carry? He should have come earlier to get a decent spot instead of letting Mum hold him up.

***

"Oh, Jess, I've put my foot in it again."

Her daughter closed the door behind her and unclipped the dog's lead.

"How's that, then?"

"I told Matt he shouldn't go out with that cold, and he snapped at me."

"And?"

"Well, I snapped back." She grimaced. "Told him it were a waste of his A-levels and there were still time to transfer to another course."

"Ah."

"He stormed out. I should've kept my mouth shut."

"It was bound to come out sometime."

"Was I that obvious?" She'd sworn not to interfere after saying something similar to her husband back when Matt was a baby. It seemed she hadn't learned much in twenty years.

"Thanks, love, for walking Tug. Do you have to get back? Or can you stay a bit?"

***

Two buskers outside the pub were casting longing glances through the window.

"If you wanna pop in for a drink," said Matt, "I can hold your spot while you're away."

The pair looked at each other. "How long are you staying?"

He shrugged. "An hour? Less if you want." He'd be happy with less.

"Sounds good to me, mate. Don't leave before we come out, though."

The singers picked up the guitar case and were gone.

Matt unstrapped his accordion. From his bag, he took a dog bowl with "Thank you" painted around it. Behind it, he propped up a sign saying donations would go to the local homeless shelter. He wasn't here for the money.

His tutor had told him he needed more "presence," whatever that was. Apparently, busking was a good experience.

At the Faculty of Performing Arts Christmas Review, he'd found that an auditorium of strangers wasn't the same as a school hall of supportive parents. Other students had covered his wobbles, but expectations would be higher next time.

His hands shook on the clips of the accordion case; he told himself it was the cold making him shiver. Lifting the heavy instrument stilled his shakes, but only on the outside.

He settled the familiar weight on his shoulders and ran his fingers across the keyboard, moving smoothly into *White Christmas*. Shoppers glanced his way. None paused.

He added flourishes to the final chorus before segueing into *The Little Drummer Boy*. This wouldn't do. He was here to sing.

He played an introduction and began, "Chestnuts roasting on an open fire," faltering at the strangled sounds that came from his throat.

Breathe. Open your throat.

"Jack Frost nipping at your TOES."

Reassured when nobody looked his way, he carried on until his voice steadied.

The playlist he'd agonised over was still in the carrier bag; its order forgotten. He'd forgotten to put coins into the dog bowl, as he'd seen other buskers do. As shoppers passed, he began to relax.

But standing out here being ignored wasn't the same as standing on a stage with everyone watching. This wouldn't conquer his stage fright. He stole a glance at his watch; how long before he could go home? He paused to adjust the instrument on his shoulders, and a woman's voice called out, "Can you do *Silent Night*, love?"

"Yeah," came a younger voice. "With sound effects."

He tensed until he spotted two women smiling at him from a nearby stall. The younger woman with the dancing eyes gave a little wave.

As he started to play, the pair stepped closer and stood swaying to *Silent Night*. He found himself swaying, too. Three children pulled their parents over to join the swaying and see the strange piano thingy. Was that someone humming along?

He broke into *Jingle Bells,* and the children sang, too. The two women started clapping, and so did others. Now, people are stopping to listen. More came. One made a request. By *Rudolph*, he was beginning to enjoy himself.

When the buskers emerged from the pub halfway through *The Twelve Days of Christmas*, they sang along. He asked if he could finish with one more song, and the children cheered.

"My grandad left me this accordion. He used to bring it out at family gatherings when I was small. He had a voice like a rusty saw, and everyone would join in to drown him out.

"The actor who sang this song couldn't sing either, but he sang it anyway in a film we watched every Christmas. This one's for Grandad."

Few children knew the words to the Muppets' *Thankful Heart,* but they recognised it and skipped to the rhythm.

The buskers took over with *Santa Claus is Coming to Town* as he packed away his accordion. When he looked up, the young woman with the dancing eyes was gone. So was her companion. The coins from the dog bowl jingled in his pocket as he hefted the accordion onto his shoulder.

Walking back through the market, the woman who had requested *White Christmas* turned away from a second-hand stall as he passed.

"Thanks, Mum," he said as she and Jess fell into step beside him.

Discussion

PHIL: "A great story, it paints the pictures beautifully. And it's the sort of thing Mums and sisters do."

DOUG: "I had to set aside two major impediments before I could concentrate on the story itself because #1 When it comes to Christmas, I make Scrooge look like a saint and #2 Like the bagpipes, a gentleman is someone who can play the accordion, but doesn't. There's a hint that Mum once risked an opinion about her husband's choices, and he took off. Apart from thinking 'good riddance,' I wondered if she really thought that what she'd said would provoke a similar reaction from Matt. Seems a little over-dramatic, especially when Matt is clearly having his own doubts about his choice of career. – I think the story would have worked better if the two women generating his audience were rugged up or disguised in some manner, and he only works it out at the end. – A dog bowl for donations to the homeless? A bit jarring. I wish Cathy every success as a writer. PS – I'll crawl back into my misanthropic cave now and eat my dinner of roast reindeer and elf pudding."

JANE: "A lovely story, and as a parent of sons, I can relate to saying the wrong thing or giving an unwanted opinion. Equally, as a mother, I always try to support them in any way I can. I really enjoyed listening to his thoughts and fears, as it made me feel I was getting to know him. (It also made me feel quite protective and sympathetic towards him) Well done, Cathy."

GEOFF: "Most enjoyable, lovely warm tale. It flows well, and you capture Matt with all his angst and frustrations very well. He has depth. Which, as Doug points out, rather contrasts with Mum and Jess. I had to re-read that little section where we get mum's POV twice in order to appreciate what was going on, and even so, I missed the bit about her 20-year-old worry at what she said to her husband. I think you'd improve the experience a little more there without compromising your neat ending. *I understand Doug's point about the fact you hid from us who they were even though Matt clearly knew, and you might have added something there – say, how his heart sank when he saw the two women and was about to give up before the one with the dancing eyes cajoled him into white Christmas. There needs to be more tension between them until it is clear their intervention and participation-singing along, clapping etc. brings in the others and gets the crowd going."

HUGH W. ROBERTS: "Well, you had me going off in a different direction with this story, Cathy. When I read the line, 'When he looked up, the young woman with the dancing eyes was gone. So was her companion,' I thought we had a Christmas ghost story on our hands and that Matt would glimpse them or find something they left behind that made him question if they had really been there, at the end of the story. So, I'd gone entirely up a different path. All in all, it is an excellent, warm, comfortable read for the festive season. It is full of nice feelings, with a bit of intrigue thrown in. Well, I was undoubtedly intrigued. I agree about how it's great to read and hear all the different directions when responding to prompts Cathy. One prompt can produce many stories, some of which can be miles apart in content. The same is true of how readers do the same thing when reading a story. Our minds are mysterious, with the results being a great discussion amongst everyone. That's where '**Story Chat**' comes into its element."

Chapter Fourteen: "When Gratitude Is Hard to Come by"

BY GEOFF LEPARD

The Ealing Invincibles are a wandering Sunday soccer team formed in 1999 by a group of actors. They play against teams across southwest London and make up for their lack of skill with unquenchable enthusiasm, a nice line in histrionics when tackled and a readiness to buy their round. If short of a player, club secretary Fergus Plaimasion sends out idiosyncratic pleas for help. For the game at Battersea Ironclads this Sunday, the message reads: *Disaster looms, motley crew. The Furies have denied us a striker and a right back. If you know of anyone waiting in the wings, bring them along.*

At 2.17 that Sunday in the shingle car park behind the dilapidated corset factory, Thoms Oldcastle's ancient VW disgorges three extras: the squat Dr Reuben Twopillow, the go-to TV medic; the tall, handsome and commanding presence of Roderick Henchbodie, currently playing Sebastián in a remake of Brideshead and mooted to be the new Darcy in Pride and Prejudice (to be shown on Sky); and his girlfriend, muse and staggeringly talented polymath, the willowy Professor Wanda Wellbedded.

Thoms does the introductions; after the ritual handshakes (for Reuben and Rod) and side-eye glances from several inherently inadequate men for Wanda, Fergus ushers the players into the changing rooms, leaving Wanda alone with her phone and a few gawping dog walkers. She barely registers their presence: having faced many university funding committees, she is more than capable of dealing with such barely disguised misogyny.

The sun peeps out despite the chill; it has all the makings of a pleasant afternoon.

An hour later, Rod waves at Fergus, who passes him the ball. He accelerates towards the goal, already considering how he will celebrate when he scores. Instead, he stumbles, and the renowned leading man leads with his famously dimpled jaw, face-planting the mud.

As is often recorded by bystanders to tragedy, time seems to slip a dimension and run slower than usual; hereabouts, it almost grinds to a halt. The other players take a moment to appreciate he has not simply tripped. Some, knowing him as an actor but not knowing the person, wonder if this is a deliberate pratfall, some comic interlude. Only two, Dr Reuben and a member of the home team, Isaac Turtle, appreciate this might be more serious than a case of befuddled feet.

They are right: Rod has suffered a catastrophic heart failure of the kind that can afflict young men, in particular during exercise and is, to all intents and purposes, dead as he hits the floor.

As the other players gather around, Reuben's instincts kick in. It may be his quick wit, formidable eyebrows and nearly packaged diversity credentials that got him the gig on TV, but he is, first and foremost, a doctor. He knows that immediate and continuous CPR is essential if his peri-deceased friend is to have a chance of living.

Isaac is a quiet young man, assumed by many to be gormless, but he is merely a watcher. This week, he has been trained in the use of the club's defibrillator. It is that he seeks as he sprints for the rickety clubhouse. With the machine clutched to his chest, he sprints back to the uniformly rapt and horrified crowd that comprises everyone, bar Wanda, who is still on her phone and oblivious to the drama unfolding behind her.

As Isaac drops to his knees and Reuben appreciates this may turn out better than he assumed moments before, the crowd seems to understand and step back. The two unexpected collaborators work in wordless harmony; soon, Reuben lifts Rod's sweaty shirt for Isaac to apply the charged paddles, once, twice, to that photogenic body.

Almost by instinct, several watchers hold their breath; it is a strange moment of solidarity with the victim. Reuben takes the pulse, leaning close.

The relief is palpable. 'He's breathing.' Moments later, he adds, 'and I can feel a pulse.'

Wanda looms over the still inert Roderick, now aware that she has almost lost her boyfriend. Her cool scientific mind manages to restrain the tsunami of emotions assaulting her. 'What happened?'

Many versions compete for her attention. She crouches at his side, instinct preventing her from dropping to her knees and potentially ruining her Gucci pantsuit. Touching her lover's cool face, he blinks. Someone cheers.

Rod is in pain and demands an explanation. 'What the bloody hell has happened to my chest?'

Reuben adopts a suitable 'don't scare the patients' manner and explains about his heart.

'Why's it hurt right the way across, then?' Before anyone can stop him, he grabs the hem and pulls his shirt to his chin, straining and failing to see the source of his discomfort.

On stage and while filming, Rod's unfeasibly beautiful and unblemished body is admired and lusted over by both men and women. He has no tattoos, but when not working, he sports two small crucifixes on nipple rings (an homage to his devout grandparents) and a silver ingot on a pendant given to him by Wanda.

The reason for Rod's discomfort is apparent to all save Rod. In applying the electrical charges, Isaac inadvertently superheated these three small metallic items, and they have burnt into Rod's taut torso.

'What's happened?' Rod takes in the sea of the faces staring at his chest. One skill that has stood him in good stead is his ability to read his audience, and, to his surprise, he detects not the expected concern but a mix of humour and pity. He forces his head higher, and despite the fact he sees an inverted version of what the others see, he realises the stark truth.

He has been branded with one word, which, once the angry, partly suppurating burns heal, will be with him forever. Any gratitude he has for his rescuers disappears as he appreciates he can never now emerge from a lake, bare-chested to woo Elizabeth Bennett. Not if all the viewers see is that one word.

TIT

Discussion

DOUG: "You are at the top of your form here, Geoff, unlike the Ealing Invincibles. Perhaps one of Dr. Twopillow's mates is a plastic surgeon, and can we lease Wodewick (apologies to Life of Brian) from his woes so he can stay abreast of Elizabeth Bennett? However, methinks that, whatever the outcome, Wanda has bigger fish to fry. And I hope that Isaac also grabbed his phone when he ran to the shed. The Sunday papers would pay handsomely for the before and after shots."

HUGH: "I had fleeting visions of a 'Carry on...' movie going through my mind as

I read Geoff's story. Very humorous, including the names of the characters, but some of the descriptions were also priceless – 'She crouches at his side, instinct preventing her from dropping to her knees and potentially ruining her Gucci pantsuit.' Thanks for the laugh, Geoff."

CATHY: "This reminds me so much of a football game in the 1970s between the admin and catering staff of a London TV company and a motley team of TV presenters and minor celebrities, although nobody expired on the pitch (or threatened to) and defibrillators wouldn't have been available if they had. My then husband was among the catering staff, and I found myself watching with the then established girlfriend of a tall, personable sports presenter whom Wanda Wellbedded brought to mind. He is still presenting – mostly quiz programmes now – but I doubt she remained his escort for long – even without the disincentive of a derogatory branding. Isaac Turtle sounded like a steady, deliberate sort of individual, and I was impressed that he managed a suitable turn of speed when retrieving the defibrillator. The final revelation had me checking back on the nipple and pendant hardware to better envisage the unplanned tattoo. I can only say... ouch! It is a lightly told tale of rescue and reserved gratitude. Nice one!"

GARY: "Geoff, this was a word-wrestling wild ride. Your names never fail to entertain, and I absolutely did not see the ending coming at all. You never fail in dragging me again to my dictionary app to see if you made up some odd onomatopoeia. The final and funny result of his rescue is where I expected to find the lack of gratitude angle, but was it not overshadowed by the visual of his branding? So, the title became a diversion to avert the reader's gaze while you built the surprise of how said branding read to any casual or interested observer. This was funny but left me trying to figure out if it would really happen this way."

Chapter Fifteen: "Handle with Caution"

BY K.L. CALEY

She stirred the tea leaves around her cup. The question mark again. She knew what that meant, "BE CAUTIOUS".

A small bird fluttered past the window and caught her eye for a second. She rose from her chair, teacup still in hand, and watched it hop around the garden. Whilst it picked up little sticks from here or there, it was cautious, always watching, always looking around. Occasionally, its stony black eyes glared directly at her, knowing she was there, yet it assessed the situation and continued as was.

The doorbell to the little shop made a noise in the background. And she hurried to tidy her cup away and make her way through the door, but before she had a chance, Tom's distinctive Scottish burr startled her.

"Reading tea leaves again, are we?"

"Always. One day, you'll let me do yours."

"Ha, you know I don't believe in all that rubbish." She laughed and then pouted, pretending to take offence. He was standing in a shop full of incense, candles, and crystals, after all.

"Then what is there to be afraid of?" She smiled, having caught him out. He raised his hands in a gesture of submission.

"I've dropped off a package for you, but this one needs a signature, I'm afraid." He gestured through the door, and she followed his gaze.

"Crikey, what's in there?" She walked over to a large box that sat in the middle of the shop floor. How strange, no return label? The neat handwritten address confirmed it was definitely for her.

"I must admit I'm curious, it's a heavy box you have there. Do you want me to give you a hand moving it?" Tom's cheerful smile seemed to sparkle off all the crystals in the room.

"Just give me two minutes, and I'll find some scissors to open it first. I can't think what it could be."

"No need, I have my pen-knife here if you want."

"Sure". She stepped back, and Tom knelt beside the box. He carefully slid his knife along the two sides and then began to slowly move down the centre seal. As he got halfway, a huge bang escaped from the box, and all the lights in the shop went out.

"Tom!" Rosie shouted into the darkness. Her eyes slowly adjusted with a little help from the LED candles scattered around the store. She could just make out Tom's body lying on the floor next to the box.

"Tom!" she shouted again, dropping to her knees beside him. His body started shaking. Then a loud noise followed.

"Hahahahaha. What the bloody hell was that? Are you trying to kill me, woman?" His deep chuckle continued to fill the air.

"Tom, it's not funny." She got back to her feet and made her way over to the lights. Expecting the fuse to be blown, she flicked them on and off, but to her surprise, the room illuminated before her. Now it was her turn to laugh. She was laughing so hard tears began streaking down her face.

"Oh, now you find it funny?" Tom asked, dusting himself off and getting to his feet. Still struggling to talk, Rosie picked up a mirror off the shelf and held it to Tom's face. He took a glance and realized he looked like a raccoon with black smudge marks around his eyes.

"So, what exactly was in that box? From the look on your face, you must have got a good look." Rosie began laughing again at her own joke.

"Well, if it was any other shop, I wouldn't believe it, but I think it's a cauldron?"

"A cauldron?" She walked over to the box, and sure enough, inside was a large black cauldron. Although more curiously, it was empty except for a small rolled-up piece of paper with a ribbon around it. Rosie unravelled it to reveal a note.

Happy Birthday, Darling, I thought you'd like this; I know you've had your eyes on it for years. I hope you didn't mind my little surprise. Lots of love, Grannie. Xx.

"You're right, it is a cauldron." She turned back to Tom and dropped the little note onto the counter. "Would you like to come through and clean yourself up a bit?"

"Yeah, if you don't mind. Perhaps I'll have that cup of tea after all." Tom added, and they made their way through to the back room. He chuckled. "I think you'll try anything to make me a believer. In saying that, I think I'll be approaching your parcels with caution from now on!"

They both laughed as Rosie put the pot on to boil. She picked her discarded teacup up to give it a rinse.

Caution. Indeed!

Discussion

GEOFF: "We then meet Tom – the postman or delivery man – and we wonder if this is the love interest's friend or arse? Tom plays dead. It's a bit childish, but whatever floats his boat. Rosie accepts his behaviour – I'd think him an arse; she doesn't – so I guess there are some feelings there. What caused the bang that leaves Tom 'racoon-faced,' and why? Grannie doesn't seem like she's grasped the concept of health and safety. He could have been blinded. No one seems to worry."

GLORIA: "I thought Tom was a threat. (Sorry, Tom) I love Grannie. I think she's a witch. This is exactly the kind of trick my dad would have played (but he wasn't a witch) with no intentions of harming anyone. I think Grannie also has a crystal ball and watches Rosie and Tom in it. She's using her magic to push them together. I think Rosie is a witch, too. White witches!"

DOUG: "Perhaps Grannie wanted to teach the poor bloke a lesson with all his Tommy rot. Poor bloke needing to be taught a lesson full of Tommyrot."

WILLOW: "Write what pleases you. Of course, read all the advice people have given, but remember you are the writer, and your opinion is key. I agree that over wordy sentences are confusing."

Chapter Sixteen:
"Sweet Feeling"

BY YVETTE PRIOR

"Slow Ride" from Foghat played on the radio as Marcel drove up the bumpy, narrow mountain road. Wondering if this strenuous drive was worth it, Marcel continued upwards. Sometimes, a sunset from what feels like the top of the world is what the soul needs.

It is like a Corpse Pose after a challenging 55-minute yoga workout. Corpse Pose does not feel quite as good unless it follows a workout. Sweetly satisfied. Or it is like watching the final episode of Breaking Bad - it only tugs at the heart - and leaves a sweet feeling - if you watch the full season leading up and ease into Baby Blue playing.

This strenuous ascent was a way for Marcel to regroup. He recently left a job that held him back like a ball and chain attached to the ankle. Now, he is still dealing with resistance as people question his choice. That drain only added to the strain of his job exit. People have good intentions. They do. Most do.

Marcel knew that this would pass. The transition would be over, and the new job would eventually sync with his identity - but handling the criticism in the meantime was like trying to extract water from a dry sponge. Marcel felt parched and done. Yet inside, he felt an ember. His inner fire almost went out the last couple of years- from feeling stuck to "being" stuck. One does not easily walk away from employment; however, when the time to break free came, it allowed his wings to stop getting clipped. It allowed that ember inside to get some fuel and to glow again.

Parking his truck, Marcel put on his gear to hike up the final three miles. He had a new song in his mind. You might think it was one of those songs about being free or coming alive. Instead, it was the lyrics to "Simple Man" that ran through his mind. "Momma told me..." played smoothly in his mind as his feet carefully maneuvered the rough terrain and switchbacks. The sounds of nature then flooded his essence, and he had that decompression of thoughts as he reached the summit.

Finding a makeshift campsite, he lightly shook the dusty poles, sipped water, hung the food bag, then zipped the tent and walked 50 feet to the cliff's edge.

There he stood and looked down - and thought of the Van Halen song - you know, "... lost a lot of friends there, baby.... I've got no time to mess around...."

Marcel wasn't messing around anymore by staying stuck.

Then

Looking up - there it was.

Right there.

Sweetness.

A mesmerizing creamsicle orange, canary yellow, and streaks of gold sunset. Hints of purple near the bottom. This phantasmagoric sunset left him speechless; it paused all thought. It was, in fact, sweeter to see a sunset from what felt like the top of the world. The physical fatigue from hiking also added to the refreshment. Funny how the human body needs stress, and it needs to be fatigued.

***

The next morning, Marcel started hiking back down before dawn. He had things to do - life was waiting to be lived - so he took sips of coffee while slowly making the descent.

As he came closer to his car, the dawn was breaking, and he lightly tripped over a rock. He reached for the branches of a dried-up shrub to try to prevent the fall, but he still landed on the ground - thump! He landed with four or five branches in his hand. He began to chuckle lightly because the toughest terrain was behind him - covered astutely, and to now take a spill on flat ground seemed humorous. Yet there he was, catching his breath and shaking off the dirt.

Looking down, Marcel noticed something. The dried-up shrub was not dead. It was dormant. There's a difference.

Inside the broken branches, he found all this bright green and white live tissue. So much life. It looked all dried up and even looked dead. But it wasn't. It was teeming with life, even if it did not appear vibrant inside. And that reminded Marcel that he, too, was not completely done. His fire would roar again.

As he brushed off the final bits of debris, he smiled at the fall. He was grateful he had this simple little stumble because there was a message he needed to take back home. He hiked to see the sunset - to be in nature - to let a challenging hike fatigue his body and refresh his soul. But he also got a little more - right near the end - and that little extra left him with a sweet feeling.

Discussion

JOY: "Great job with the story! Good point about the body needing a certain amount of fatigue. I also loved your line about dormant, not meaning that you're dead and pointing out that his fire will burn again. There was hope throughout this story. Maybe Marcel didn't have it all figured out, but he was taking a step, and there was a sweetness in that. Keep writing, eager to see what comes next!"

GARY: "Hi Yvette, Welcome to the monthly spotlight. "Sweet Feeling" left me with exactly that; a very sweet feeling after reading it. I thought the image of Marcel working his way up the road, getting bumped around, set a good tone of, 'Is this really worth the effort – I want it to be, but I don't want to destroy my car in the process. Yvette, you are an artist. I feel like I shared this man's trip and now his memory. What I like best about this **Story Chat** phenomenon is how well we got to know each other and what we're thinking when we write. This is almost as good as chatting in person with our own real coffee mugs in hand, laughing, probing, encouraging, and, yes, you are correct, learning things along the way. Friends read each other, but really good ones add some polish as they pass through the virtual rooms we live in."

NORAH: "What a lovely story. My mind raced into all sorts of places as I read, but the story didn't follow me anywhere. It was a sweet ending to a story that I thought may have been tragic. Why would I expect something sinister from you?"

LINDA: "Yvette, I enjoyed Marcel's journey out in nature, losing himself, just like you and I also do when hiking in nature. I cringed when he stumbled and was happy he was able to go on refreshed and ready to take on the world again. Forget about what the others say about his decision... he is his own man, and just as we should all be doing."

HUGH: "A sweet story. I thought it told a great lesson that life isn't always playing out the way we think it is. I've had many incidents when I thought the whole world was against me, but then I encounter or hear something that makes me think that things aren't that bad and that it is far better than what some people are going through. I thought Marcel would jump off that cliff, so I was relieved all he was doing was checking out the sunset and that the fall he did have gave him new hope."

Chapter Seventeen:
"The Power of Verticality"

BY ANNE GOODWIN

I had a husband once. Sisters. Friends. One by one, they fell away like petals from a daisy. She loves me. She loves me not. She comes. She goes.

She arrives hot-breathed, panting. Tobacco habit? Angina? Lift on the blink and too many stairs? It hurts my head to contemplate the options, the galaxy of possibilities within the world outside.

Inevitably, she carries fragments of the vast beyondness. The scent of mint from her toothpaste. The patina of mist in her hair. The power of verticality. The rough chill of her hands.

Mostly, she brings words. Words from her heart and words she read from the screen of her phone or from print.

She claims these words are helping me. I mustn't lose touch with current affairs. Yet she forgets her reading glasses, and even with them, she muddles Dhaka and Dakar, Slovakia and Slovenia, Uruguay and Paraguay. Worse, as the story nears its climax, she buries it in her bag. "You're getting agitated. Let's have a nice cup of tea."

She brings a thermos, a rusty canister from summer picnics long ago. She brings a thermos because no one makes tea the way she drinks it. The way tea is meant to be. She pours one for me "to be sociable." When it's grown cold sitting on the locker, she drains it down the sink.

Sometimes, she reads aloud from women's glossies. Make-up tips and mindfulness and how to tell if he's the one. In my dreams, I check the dictionary to separate *ironic* and *incongruous* from *malicious* and *sly*.

She reminds me she's all I've got now. Of course, she doesn't count the staff. Once there were doctors and specialist nurses, as hope peeled away, status went with it, like dead skin. Now, there are women with brisk hands and tilted English, strong women supporting three generations in another continent on the minimum wage. She slows her voice to speak to them, and it's always to complain.

She doesn't like the gown I'm in. It's too tight, too loose, too bright, too pale. She says she'll bring a better one tomorrow. Threat or promise, who's to know? Tomorrow never happens. Or M&S failed to stock the thing she had in mind. Relief or disappointment? Too late for us to learn respect for each other's styles.

In her custody, my preferences are weaponised to undermine the staff. "She wouldn't want her hair like that," she says. "Easy listening? She'd rather have a rock."

When she's not here, the staff plays eerie instrumentals from their home countries or upbeat singalongs stuffed with unfamiliar words. The only way I know it's night is when chat and music surrender to the murmur of machines.

Alone with me, she lifts the sheet and digs her nails into my thigh. She closes in to shout obscenities in my ear. If caught, she'd say I need the stimulation. She's the key that will unlock me from this limbo. She's always cast her cruelty as maternal love.

Once, we shared a body. Now, we share this cocoon. She makes the boundary blur between me and not me. My brain betrays me: Did *she* nurse *me* through infancy, or did *I* nurse *her*? *Mother* and *daughter* are words I recognise but I don't know which belongs to me. When we merge, I can't distinguish *trapped* from *free*.

Daughters visit ailing *mothers*, I reason. It's the natural way. So, when she pats my hand and says it's time to go, I believe *I'll* drive back to my husband, sisters, and friends.

She bends to kiss my cheek. "See you tomorrow, darling."

Inside my shell, I scream with rage and disappointment. Because I'll miss her? Because I envy her? Because she promised to come back?

Discussion

K. L.: "I guess we are lured into trusting most narrators, but with this one, we know we can't as she can't be too sure herself who she is. I would say she is Naively Unreliable: a Narrator who is honest but lacks all the information. They simply lack a traditional, "greater understanding.""

CATHY: "The story is a mystery, almost poetically framed. Mention of the 'world outside' is our first clue, described as a 'vast beyondness.'

- Her visitor has the 'power of verticality' that provides our title, so it must be significant.

- Having staff suggests a care home or a hospice. 'Hope peeled away ... like dead skin', along with her status, reveals her feeling of worthlessness. She has nothing to give back. But, helpless, she is unable to respond anyway – not even to pinches and obscenities.

- Maternal love is cited, but even the protagonist isn't sure which of them is the mother. Trapped inside her own head, is she the daughter trapped in a coma? (a disappointment to her mother due to drugs or other failures) or – more likely, I think – a mother floundering in the fog of Alzheimer's?

- Information is gradually released in a masterful way, but still, nothing is certain – as the protagonist is no

longer certain of anything.
Very well done!

CHARLI: "The agony of not being able to communicate is keenly felt in those last three questions. Ah! This is why I love Anne's writing. She allows readers the space to experience the inner world of another with no right or wrong interpretation. We are left with an alternative to "the end." Anne gives us a chance to withdraw from "this is." And as readers, we leave, but continue to mull over what we bore witness to."

ROBBIE: "This is a story that makes you think. At first, I thought they could be sisters who still had some sibling rivalry between them. Now, I think it is a mother and daughter who might not have had a strong relationship. One character is trapped in her body, unable to respond or care for herself. The other character takes advantage of the condition. It's like she is getting revenge while showing false concern. She is enjoying the control she has over the first character."

Chapter Eighteen:
"As Far As a Former Prisoner Can Go"

BY CHARLI MILLS

James found out how far gate money would get him from the state prison in Sacramento. When the bus pulled into a convenience store after midnight, he thought its name was funny – Kum & Go. It wasn't until the bus driver yelled, "Paulina!" that James realized he'd reached the destination on his ticket. He slid out of his seat, grabbed his paper bag, and walked to the front, envying the sleeping passengers.

"Where's the town?" James asked.

"This is Paulina, Iowa." The driver made notations into an electronic device.

"It's a gas station in the middle of tall grass."

The driver snorted. "If you haven't ever seen corn before, you'll get an eyeful here."

James left the bus and faced the gloom at the edge of fluorescent lights. The bus door was sealed, and the engine spewed diesel fumes. Silence. Darkness. The despair of solitary confinement settled over him like the smell of rot.

How long he stood there, James couldn't say. His thoughts lingered on coffee, but he'd spent all the $200 they gave him for leaving prison. He hadn't counted on an isolated destination.

Tires crunched gravel scattered across the pavement, and James shuddered, staying small in the shadows. A black Ford truck with shiny rims swung into the gas station, pulling up to the pumps. The driver stepped out and spotted James like a seasoned warden. He dropped his eyes in deference to the authority of the stranger, but not before catching a glimpse of blonde hair from within the cab. James snapped his head back up, eyes wide, mouth slack.

"You gonna rob the place?" the man asked.

James stammered, searching for words.

"Or maybe you think you can rob me, the dude with no legs."

James realized the man stood on two prosthetics beneath his khaki cargo shorts. The man's t-shirt stretched across a broad chest and proclaimed, "NO ONE DIED." US ARMY and American flag decals decorated the back window. It all made sense. For the first time in two years, James felt a flutter of hope. He dropped to his knees and cried out, "Buttercup!"

A yellow lab leaped from the front seat, wiggled from wet nose to feathery tail, and encircled James. He laughed and cried as the dog's tongue slopped across his face. A sharp whistle and the dog loped back to the man at the truck.

The gas pump ticked like a clock while the man finished filling his tank.

James met the stranger's gaze. "You served in Iraq." It wasn't a question.

The man nodded. "How do you know my dog?"

"I trained her. In prison. Two years ago, she was placed with a wounded soldier."

The man walked over and offered James a hand up. "Two years ago, that dog gave me a new life."

James felt his throat thicken. He nodded. "I've missed her."

"When did you get out?"

"Three days ago. This was as far as I could get with a bus ticket."

"What the hell kind of badass prisoner names a dog 'Buttercup'?"

James grinned and tipped back his head. "She was the sweetest puppy any of us had ever seen. Kind eyes. Soft hair. The color of meadow flowers. Something better than concrete, gangs, and drugs. We whispered 'Buttercup' like a prayer."

The man grunted. "Well, Buttercup and I are on our way to help build tiny houses for homeless vets in Kansas City. At least three other vets involved with the project have dogs from the prison program. We've been talking about starting one of our own."

"A service dog program?"

"Yeah. You trained a good dog. Could you train more?"

Once again, Buttercup gave James the chance to be human.

Discussion

ANNE: "I don't like dogs or happy endings, but I really enjoyed this story of redemption. I take the points made by other readers about some of the details and coincidences, but was too wrapped up in the emotion to notice. I laughed when Buttercup turned out to be a dog – I wasn't expecting that. I could totally believe he was spending all his money on the bus ticket – for me, it demonstrates his lack of preparation for the outside world, and you can't help worrying about how he'll manage. Plus, it reminded me of Jane Eyre: when she flees Thornfield after the aborted wedding, she leaves herself destitute by splurging all her cash on a coach ride as far away as she can. Sometimes people make bad decisions."

COLLEEN: Charli's story had me in tears. I loved the synchronicity of new beginnings in her story. When I read a short piece of fiction, I don't want any loose ends. I love that life seemed to come full circle for this prisoner and vet. I'll have a go at the story to see what flows forth from the muse… ♥

ROBERTA: This is a lovely story that ends on a positive note. Dogs and other animals are very therapeutic, and it is nice to read about the love of an animal, leading to a second chance for a person.

JO: "I know it's irrelevant, but I wanted to know why he was a prisoner."

MICHAEL: "I love just about anything that illustrates the coincidences we have all around us in life (if we notice them), so I very much liked that James got off of the bus in the town that Buttercup ended up in. How do you explain something like that? You can't, and that's the beauty of things like that."

Chapter Twenty:
"Not a Proper Job"

BY PHILIP CUMBERLAND

The guided bus was an unusual getaway vehicle, but it had served Sheila well in the past.

It's their vanity that makes them vulnerable, she thought. What dignitary full of importance could refuse an honorary doctorate from one of the World's leading universities?

"More wine, Mr. Ambulant? Yes, the glass is a bit dirty. I will fetch you a clean one, it was the Chardonnay, wasn't it?"

Fortunately, Sheila was in the kitchen and nowhere near Mr. Ambulant when he collapsed. When they all rushed to see what was happening, she was in the ladies' room, changing out of the waitress's uniform into jeans and a tee shirt. Nipping out through the Master's Garden was a bit naughty, really, but not as naughty as poisoning someone. Thank goodness for the tourists. It was easy to get swallowed up by the crowds.

The bus was waiting in its bay when she arrived at Drummer Street. Some of those academics can be a bit handy when a girl is carrying a tray of drinks in a fairly short skirt. Women were the worst.

Had she been missed yet? The thought crossed her mind.

The Park and Ride is very useful. You can park for free, get into the middle of Cambridge, and then come back to pick your car up. The luggage lockers are useful, too; the jiffy bag was waiting for her in one. Sheila would check its contents later; no doubt instructions for the next job were in there, too.

The policemen standing waiting by her car were a surprise. She noticed them as she closed the locker door. It is always sensible to park near the bus shelter. Fortunately, the bus was still waiting to move on. She climbed back on, flashed her day rider ticket at the driver, and found a seat next to the emergency exit. As she left the bus at Huntingdon, she thought it was always good to have a plan B. Her backup, an elderly Renault Clio, was inconspicuous and could be left anywhere without arousing suspicion, provided there were no yellow lines or parking restrictions.

She drove to her cottage in nearby Wistow. It wasn't her main address, but somewhere out of the way when life got complicated. With a wry smile on her face, she opened the Chardonnay, poured herself a glass, and reached for the Jiffy bag. Inside were a few hundred, in twenty and ten-pound notes for expenses. The lottery ticket was there, too. The photograph of her next target was a bit of a surprise. He was nasty and odious enough but well connected.

He must have really upset someone, Sheila thought, and then she remembered a story, well, a rumour of a story, which would explain it. No matter how big a bully you are, there is always someone bigger and nastier.

Right, London on Monday to claim her lottery prize and perhaps a call to Grandmother. The Sunday papers headlined Ambulant's sudden death; a heart attack was the suspected cause; the college had secured the endowment before his demise.

Sunday passed quietly. It was the eleven-thirty train from Huntingdon on Monday that delivered Sheila to Kings Cross.

Discussion

CATHY: "Lots of local colour in here: Cambridge's controversial but now widely used guided bus, the park-and-ride car parks, bits of the university and, of course, the tourists. For those wondering about the lottery ticket, collecting her winnings is the means by which payment is made. One can't help but wonder at the connections of the paymaster to be able to engineer a lottery win at will (always assuming that this is our National Lottery and not a smaller-scale lottery. In the UK, such lesser lotteries would probably not pay out a large enough sum without comment)."

GEOFF: "The lottery ticket had me wondering how this could be used for payment. I doubt Camelot is beyond corruption, but still! The bus also confused me in that I imagined an open-top to be a tourist bus, but it appeared to double as a park and ride. Did I miss something? Maybe it doesn't matter, but it distracted me. Sheila took us on a bit of a ride. If she is a competent assassin – which seems a fair assumption if she's getting an immediate second commission – how can the police trace her to her car so fast? I'd love to think Cambridgeshire's Finest was that good... So, she left a clue as to where she was going, did she? Or were they there for another reason? It's a highly enjoyable tale of callousness wrapped up in domesticity, but the above, for me, disrupted the flow, which was a shame."

GLORIA: "Sheila reminds me of the character Villanelle in 'Killing Eve'. Villanelle is a totally ruthless assassin who would perform jobs just like this one, being very well disguised for each one. She would receive instructions for her next job in a similar way to Sheila, also with a photo of her next victim. Never with a lottery ticket, though. I paused when I got to the ticket part... I thought I missed something at the start and scrolled back to check. 'Some of those academics can be a bit handy when a girl is carrying a tray of drinks in a fairly short skirt. Women were the worst.' This line was lost on me, I'm afraid. I've no idea what it means or how it fits into the story. I couldn't figure out why Mr Ambulant was killed. Something to do with the university, I think. He obviously wronged someone somewhere... Because the TV series Killing Eve is etched in my mind, I think that Sheila's grandmother might have a past of her own and could give Sheila a few tips on how to be a great assassin! Maybe Grandma is her employer. Hee hee! Not all elderly women are sweet little ladies! Thanks for the intriguing story, Philip. Looking forward to connecting with you on your blog and reading more of your stories."

HUGH: "Loved reading this short piece about Sheila. She reminded me so much of a female James Bond. I think nobody will ever be able to trace her because any CCTV will be wiped by the government. As for the lottery ticket as payment, I'm convinced somebody rigs the numbers on each draw, probably the government, so it's a great way of them paying somebody who needs to be off the radar and never have to record wages. A delightful read, Philip."

Chapter Twenty-One:
Backstab

BY GLORIA MCBREEN

"Do you feel bitter about not being able to have children?" Millie asked her sister.

Judy bit her lip. "When I said I couldn't have children, I meant that I couldn't bring children into a life of corruption and debauchery."

Millie's jaw dropped. "You lied?"

"No, I misled. There's a difference. Letting people think I was infertile meant I didn't have to endure constant criticism and opinions."

"You could've told me."

"No, Millie. Because I would've had to tell you everything, and I couldn't back then. Anyway, I'm only 38."

Millie beamed. "You mean there's still a chance that I'll become an Auntie?"

Judy grinned and raised her eyebrows. "Let's sit on the balcony." She slid her white Gucci sunglasses from her head to the bridge of her nose.

As the sisters settled into their sun loungers, Judy marvelled at the acres of lavender before them. She was proud of Millie and the good life she had made for herself in their ancestral homeland. She had worked hard to establish her career as a psychotherapist. Her French husband Leo, a pharmacist, doted on her and their two young sons. They deserved their comfortable lifestyle—unlike her. But things are different now. Judy had a new purpose in life.

"Which were you most attracted to...Lucas or the lifestyle?" Millie asked.

"I loved him first, and then I fell in love with his wealth. More the security of it, though. The lavish lifestyle was attractive, sure, but I realised it wasn't for me."

"You hated all those parties, though. Why did you continue going to them after you found out how Lucas really made his money?

Judy enjoyed the parties and charity events at first. But when the novelty of being a rich man's wife wore off a few months into the marriage, she began to notice things. The women at the parties who flirted with Lucas. The way he responded to them, in front of her, as if she—his wife— didn't exist. He was a different man at those ritzy parties than he was at his charity events.

But it was the younger women that Judy took more notice of. They were at all the parties, with different men each time. Floozies, she used to call them. On the surface, they seemed to be enjoying themselves, but Judy looked deeper.

It was in their eyes, their body language. She noticed how they silently communicated with each other. Things weren't right! Lucas never engaged with the young girls. He preferred the more mature women—the diamond-clad types, who seemed to sweat Chanel and Estée Lauder. Bit by bit, Judy picked and peeled at the layers of every aspect of Lucas Lambert.

"It was at those parties I learned all about my sleazy husband and his money-making endeavours."

Millie took a bottle of Pinot Grigio from an ice bucket and poured two glasses. The late afternoon sun shone directly onto the balcony. She put on her wide-brimmed hat to shade her nurtured complexion.

"I never liked him, Judy. I had a gut feeling about him from the beginning. Slimeball! I hope he's experiencing hell right now." Millie took a generous sip of her chilled wine. 'How did you stay after you found out about those poor girls?"

"He wouldn't have let me leave. I suffered one hiding from him, and I wasn't prepared to give him an excuse to do it again. It was like his charity events, put in place to create a false impression, part of his façade. The timid, ordinary-looking wife, sensible shoes, and a natural ability to melt into her surroundings."

Judy massaged sun cream vigorously into her pale, pudgy legs.

"He didn't know his wife very well at all, did he?"

"He hadn't a clue what I was up to while he was off gallivanting with his rich women and drug-dealing buddies. All that was bad enough, Millie, but trafficking young women sickened me to the core. I couldn't let him continue."

"And George?" Millie asked with a cheeky grin.

Judy felt a warm blush tingle down her neck. She and Lucas' accountant, George, had become more than just conniving partners.

"This time next week, you'll get to meet him. I knew he wasn't like Lucas and the others. I knew I could trust him."

"You took a risk."

"I had a gut feeling about him, the way you had about Lucas. It's not easy moving millions around banks. I couldn't have done that part without George. We knew the Criminal Assets Bureau would be all over Lucas as soon as the filth hit the merry-go-round. It was all hard work, you know; virtually putting people in places where we needed them to be, then putting them there in real life—that was the hardest part. All those party people stoned on coke and cocktails, guiding me all the way through the labyrinth...without even realising it with their loose, inebriated tongues and their attention-craving egos. They taught me all the ins and outs of the business, as they called it. I developed valuable skills, Millie. I fluffed up more egos than pillows in the last two years."

Judy wasn't ashamed that she was a thief and a backstabber. It was all to save women from people like Lucas. To the left of the lavender field, she could see the roof of her new women's refuge centre. The skylight opened just as she left it to let the floral scent waft through her and George's apartment. Three young women she brought with her from Dublin were already settled in downstairs.

"We'll support you running the centre, Judy."

"I know it won't be easy. I've been working on my French, too."

"Merveilleux!" Millie praised.

Judy raised her glass. "Here's to Lucas and his seedy friends repenting behind bars for the rest of their lives."

"Wondering who stitched them up," laughed Millie.

"And here's to all the women who come my way," Judy smiled.

Discussion

GEOFF: "It's an interesting premise that raises many questions about how Judy and George unpicked this criminal operation and yet remained undiscovered while the protagonists were appropriately dealt with; that's probably for the book that will follow this teaser! It's set delightfully with some great imagery, the description of the lavender, the pillows, etc. There are some personal snippets of the two women – pudgy legs – but I would have liked a little more. I'd love a little more of an explanation about the ancestral home; I think the timing might need some work. At the outset, Millie clearly knows some, but not a lot, of Judy's backstory, yet the women's shelter has been set up and its first occupants installed. Wouldn't these sorts of details have been revealed over previous glasses of something chilled and white?

Millie appears to have a stable situation and a classically comfortable life. As such, she doesn't express much of the worry she must have felt for her sister caught up with someone so dodgy. And did she try to pass on those feelings, and was she pushed away and hurt?"

CATHY: "It is a challenge to cut down a story to 1,000 words without missing out on some of the backgrounds. You, as the writer, know what happens, so you tend to forget the reader doesn't if one hasn't told them. On the other hand, it's good to leave something to the readers' imagination. I love that you confess you didn't want to go into how the villain was taken down because you didn't know – I feel the same way about detective fiction. Although it's what we watch most on TV, I've never tried to write any. There is plenty in here for the reader to speculate about, as has been mentioned above. Not a lot of description of the women, but my imagination tells me that Judy's pudgy legs could be a symptom of not looking after herself in the hope her husband would leave her alone in favour of those rich older women. Perhaps a mention of her having come from Dublin earlier on might have helped anchor us without giving too much away, but I'm just niggling."

YVETTE: "I think it was interesting the way you anchored with various ethical considerations. The opening deception: the topic of childbearing fertility – and added in the justification and societal issues (how astute) and then had the backstabbing deception that then had serious outreach for victims of trafficking."

GLORIA: "My brain seems to automatically shift back a few decades when I write stories. The Internet and mobile phones rarely feature in my tales. We did have computers, but it was 1991 before the Internet came to Ireland. So, I'd imagine it would have been easier for the account to embezzle from Lucas. And easier to hide away afterward, i.e., no social media. Back in the 80s/90s, I remember Estee Lauder being worn only by well-off women. I was in my mid-20s when I got a bottle of Chanel No 5. Well...I thought I was the Queen Bee! I choose Pinot Grigio as it would be a wine I would like to drink on a sunny patio looking out onto a field of lavender!"

Chapter Twenty-Two: A Daily Regret

BY GARY A. WILSON

"Let me start the recording." CLICK

"This is Tom Deerling, and today I'm interviewing Reggie Mattox, the renowned creator and CEO of Cynosure Artisans. Thanks for speaking with me, Mr. Mattox. I can promise you that all my followers know your name and how you created the wildly successful, privately held Cynosure Artisans. You've launched the careers of thousands of artists and raised the bar for other media houses. The story of how you created and grew CA to its present state is now very well known, so, as agreed, let's explore something different. You've been very successful, but no one is exempt from real life. I think my followers would like to know if you have any regrets – anything you would do differently if you could go back and change something."

"Thanks, Tom. To make sure we're clear with your audience, we agreed to this question in advance, giving me time to think it through, and you've agreed to publish the interview, as delivered, with no edits, thus the recording."

"All correct. We did, and I look forward to hearing what you're willing to share."

"Very well." [deep breath] "I admit, I struggled with this but came to a perspective that I'm willing to detail. Okay, let's do this. I do have one big regret.

"I'm older now, and these days, I live a quiet and reasonable lifestyle, but that was not always the case. I was out of control when I was younger."

"Ah – yes. There have been, shall we say, more than a few tabloid stories and..."

"Ugh – let's not discuss those – they are humiliating now because I know I deserve most of what was written. Let's just say that I was a heavy partier, abused alcohol and recreational drugs, and had inappropriate relations with too many women. It's all true, and I own it. But Tom, I want your followers to know, if they care, that I'm not that man any longer, and I regret my previous life."

"Wow – um, Mr. Mattox. I did not see this coming. Your reputation has always been defensive if asked about these things."

"Well, I had to talk myself into sharing it, but it was the first thing that came to mind when you offered this interview. I wanted to find something less embarrassing, but my biggest regret is the emotional damage I left in my wake and the price I'm now paying. You see, I have a brother..."

"Ethan – yes. He works near San Francisco doing IT something, correct?"

"Correct. He has a wonderful family who are so special to me, partially because he did life right and has the rewards to show for it. My nephew and nieces are priceless joys – every time I'm with them.

In my life, that is, my previous life, there was one woman and relationship that was worth anything, and I walked away from it – from her. You might have read about Amelia. She and I were briefly together in Denver when I was starting Cynosure Artisans. She was an amazing singer with one of the bands. She was also smart and kind and – and I never should have let her go. Instead, I went on to make myself sick."

"Sick? I don't think we've heard about..."

"You would not have. It was so embarrassing; I kept it quiet. [deep breath] Tom, I caught a nasty venereal disease, and it left me sterile. I can't have children of my own. What I caught was treatable, but I hid the fact for too long and by the time I took it seriously, the damage was permanent."

"Mr. Mattox – I'm sorry to learn of this, but my followers – they'll want to know – what did you catch?"

"I hate that I know this name by heart, but it was *Neisseria gonorrhoeae*, a nasty bacteria better known as gonorrhea. Even if there were a cure for me now, I'm too old to have and raise children, so I focus on my business and try to live a quieter life."

"And Amelia? What became of her?"

"As I recall, she was devastated when I told her I was moving on without her. I had parties to see, other women to bed, other heights to reach. I know she would still hate me, so I don't know where she is, but now, barely a day goes by that I don't think of her."

"Mr. Mattox – I don't know how to proceed. You've completely blown me off course with this regret."

"Please, Tom, I've been presuming on your willingness to be referred to by your first name all along. I apologize. It's something of an artifact of my position – a bad habit I'm still trying to unwind. Please call me Reggie."

"Um – well – let me think. Ugh, no, I don't think I can call you by your first name. I had an ulterior motive for asking for this interview and think it would be wrong for me to address you so."

"Why's that? I've been honest with you, and I think..."

"That's just it. I believe you have been honest with me and my followers. I wasn't expecting anything like this and needed to rethink how... I need to step up to your honesty and match it with my own.

"You see, my father left my mom in the same way that you left Amelia. She was devastated, found that she was pregnant with me, never married, but focused on raising me and carving out the best life she could for us. She was honest with me about my father and was, and she still is, an amazing mother."

“I’m sorry to hear this, but...”

“So – I can’t call you Reggie, sir. I should not even be calling you Mr. Mattox. I need to both address you by your proper title of – of Dad and tell you that Mom would love to hear from you.”

Discussion

LISA: "Wow, I first mused that the interviewee agreed to be interviewed in an effort to "get *her* back." And then the hidden intention of the interviewer was revealed! Never read anything like it. Yes, I, too, have known many Reggies and many men & women who have lived with relationship regrets for most of their lives. The carelessness with which we can treat each other is sad, really. I've never read anything where such long-held, deep desires were publicly revealed by two male characters in such a short space of time."

K.L.: "You did a great job of transitioning both characters' POV (point of view) in such a short piece. It's quite easy for the readers to picture themselves falling into that situation and becoming rather tongue-tied. I liked the dialogue writing structure; I found it very refreshing. One of my favourite lecturers once said, 'If you can write dialogue, you can write,' meaning that it's very hard to capture authentic dialogue. It can sound too much like an extract from a textbook (his example was – would you fall off a cliff and shout... excrement – No, you'd probably use a rather more foul form of the word! Lol). Or it can go the other way and sound too fake, making you think that no one talks like that. I think you capture dialogue very well. I think the father's reveal was handled really well. The interviewer was clearly expecting the interviewee to be as per the tabloids and wanted a confrontation, but when presented with a softer side to him, it changed his perception, and I think that reflects real life well. We can't trust everything we read in the tabloids, and even if it is the truth at the time, people do learn, grow and reflect. You've captured that well here."

ROBERTA: "I thought this was a very good story. It is quite odd that I should read it this week as on Wednesday, I had a conversation with my 83-year-old mother about regrets. She said that as you get older, you have regrets about things you did in your life that hurt other people or failed to support them. I do think that if you have something big in your past, like the event detailed in this story, you would feel regret, especially if you ended up all alone with no one who cared about you. I think there are a lot of lonely older men and women out there who made mistakes that cost them the love of their families. I also don't have personal experience with this. I have wonderful parents."

YVETTE: "That was such a delightful ending that earned the heart! Reggie's maturity and openness felt so realistic, and I could imagine his eyes getting wet right after the big reveal of being a dad (especially after thinking that was not ever an option for him). It really did work (dialogue). Oh, and the dialogue-only part also felt culturally timely because podcasts seem to be huge right now (and I guess before that, we had decades of radio). But the interview felt so real."

GLORIA: "Tom's ulterior motive for the interview was to confront Reggie about Amelia and to reveal that he's his son. Or did he want to interview him only because he's his son but only decided to reveal that information after Reggie's honest admissions? As it's a recording, it's not like a live interview, so Reggie wouldn't have to agree to it being published.

Another thought I had was that both men knew the truth about the parentage before the interview and went public with the information as a publicity stunt. I wouldn't be a fan of Reggie's lifestyle, but I had a little 'aww' moment when Tom said that Amelia would like to meet him. Everyone deserves a wee bit of happiness, especially when they show remorse for their wrongdoings. I enjoyed this story, Gary. Getting so many details to us in the form of an interview was a clever idea."

AUTHOR BIOS

Hugh W. Roberts

Hugh W. Roberts lives in Swansea, South Wales, in the United Kingdom. Hugh gets his inspiration for writing from various avenues, including writing prompts, photos, eavesdropping and while out walking his dogs, Toby and Austin. Although he was born in Wales, he has lived around various parts of the United Kingdom, including London, where he lived and worked for 27 years.

Hugh suffers from a mild form of dyslexia but, after discovering blogging, decided not to allow the condition to stop his passion for writing. Since creating his blog 'Hugh's Views & News' in February 2014, he has built up a strong following and now writes every day. Always keen to promote other bloggers, authors and writers, Hugh enjoys the interaction blogging brings and has built up a group of online friends he considers as an 'everyday essential.' His short stories have become well known for the unexpected twists they contain in taking the reader up a completely different path than the one they think they are on.

One of the best compliments a reader can give Hugh is, **"I never saw that ending coming."** Having published his first book of short stories, Glimpses, in December 2016, his second collection of short stories, More Glimpses, was released in March 2019.

A keen photographer, he also enjoys cycling, walking, reading, watching television, and enjoys relaxing with a glass of red wine and sweet popcorn. Hugh shares his life with John, his civil partner, and Toby and Austin, their Cardigan Welsh Corgis.

***

MARSHA INGRAO

She lives in Prescott, AZ, with her husband and cat Moji. Marsha Ingrao retired from education as a history and math consultant after teaching elementary students for nearly ten years. After retirement, she began blogging in 2012, which opened a host of new opportunities. In 2015, Arcadia Books published her book Images of America Woodlake.

She loves blogging, photography, traveling, and walking at least 10,000 steps a day. Other favorite pastimes include working jigsaw puzzles, cooking, writing curriculum for Bible studies, and socializing. She and her husband manage the rental of their vacation condo in Scottsdale, AZ. They always have a remodeling project going somewhere.

***

CATHY CADE

Most of the time, she lives with her husband and dogs in Cambridgeshire's Fenland. The rest of the time, they live across a fence from London's Epping Forest.

Cathy Cade is a former librarian who enjoyed solving puzzles in retirement. She began writing to exercise the other side of her brain (the side that can't find the word she wants) and now has little time for puzzles. She is also an expert on commas.

All of her stories are available online from Smashwords and your local Amazon. Her story-verse, *A Year Before Christmas,* Her collection of short stories: *Witch Way, and other ambiguous stories,* an alternative Cinderella, and *Pond People* about the Mirlings that live in the fishpond.

***

ANNE GOODWIN

Away from her desk, Anne guides book-loving walkers through the Derbyshire landscape that inspired Charlotte Brontë's Jane Eyre.

Anne Goodwin's drive to understand what makes people tick led to a career in clinical psychology. That same curiosity now powers her fiction.

Anne writes about the darkness that haunts her and is wary of artificial light. She makes stuff up to tell the truth about adversity, creating characters to care about and stories to make you think. She explores identity, mental health and social justice with compassion, humour and hope.

A prize-winning short-story writer, she has published three novels and a short story collection with a small independent press, Inspired Quill. Her debut novel, *Sugar and Snails*, was shortlisted for the 2016 Polari First Book Prize.

Anne Goodwin is the author of two novels and a short story collection. "A Postcard from the Past" is based on a scene from one of many drafts of her debut novel, *Sugar and Snails*. *Sugar and Snails* was published by Inspired Quill in 2015 and shortlisted for the Polari First Book Prize.

***

GEOFF LE PARD

Le Pard lives in and loves London.

Geoff Le Pard was born in 1956 and is a lawyer who saw the light and started writing in 2006 following a summer school course. As a course junkie, he has tried Arvon, a Birkbeck College evening class and summer school and, latterly, an MA at Sheffield Hallam.

Le Pard has many likes and interests, including cooking, a passion for walking with dogs and exploring the outside world as he ponders his life. He enjoys toiling as a jobbing gardener under the Textiliste's careful instruction, reading of the good, the bad and the indifferent in fiction. As the boy's Scout picture above suggests, Le Pard volunteers his time. He follows many sports (as long as no horses are involved); Darkened theaters and cinemas draw him in as he hopes that he is exhilarated and not anaesthetised. He also enjoys dancing, both ballroom and Latin.

***

DOUG JACQUIER

Doug Jacquier lives with his wife, Sue, in Yankalilla.

He writes stories and poems. He's a father and grandfather, an avid cook, vegetable gardener and incurable punster, as well as an occasional stand-up comedian.

He's had over 30 jobs (including rock band roadie) and has lived in many places across Australia, including regional and remote communities.

Doug has travelled extensively, especially in Asia, the US and the UK. He's a recovering social worker and former not-for-profit CEO and has now retired to the real world.

He's had his work included in several anthologies, including New Poets 21, Indigo Mania, Ship Street Poetry and On The Premises. He contributes regularly to writing blogs, including Carrot Ranch and Blog Battle. His aim is to surprise, challenge and amuse.

***

ANNE STORMONT

Although she has lived in Scotland all her life, Anne is well-travelled, having visited every continent except Antarctica.

Anne Stormont is a Scot and is the author of four contemporary romantic novels – one is a standalone, and the other three make up the Skye series. The books are all second-chance romances where the main characters may be older but are certainly no wiser.

She has also published one children's novel under the name of her alter-ego, Anne McAlpine.

She began making up stories as a child to entertain her four wee sisters. But as an adult with a busy life as a mother and teacher, it took her a long time and a bit of a dramatic wake-up call for her to get that first book written. Anne is currently writing a new novel set in the Scottish Borders.

When she's not writing, Anne enjoys reading – a lot – yoga, walking and gardening. She can be a bit of a subversive old bat, but she tries to maintain a kind heart. She also loves tea, penguins and spending precious time with her friends and family.

***

DEBBIE HARRIS

Debbie has recently turned 60, is a mother of 3 grown up daughters, Granny Debs, to 4 grandchildren, married for 41 years, lived in Tumbarumba (NSW Australia) for 30 years and is happy to stay there for the foreseeable future.

A tragic accident at age 17, resulting in a Bravery Award from the Queen, didn't deter Debbie from travelling the world. A young retiree, after being made redundant from her 22-year career managing education programs in a men's correctional centre, she now happily spends her time reading, writing, blogging, riding her ebike, volunteering for a variety of community groups and is a proud Rotarian and enjoys a good cup of tea! Life is never dull.

***

GARY ARTHUR WILSON

***

CHARLI MILLS

Charli Mills, a born buckaroo, is the award-winning goat-tying champion of a forgotten 1970s rodeo. Now, she wrangles words. Married to a former US Army Ranger, Charli Mills is "true grit" but not John Wayne. She writes about the veteran spouse experience and gives voice to women and others marginalized in history, especially on frontiers.

In 2014, she founded an imaginary place called Carrot Ranch where real literary artists could gather. As lead buckaroo, she's crafted and compiled enough flash fiction to understand its value. Charli Mills developed the Congress of the Rough Writers to collaborate with flash fiction writers from Carrot Ranch.

Charli hosts a literary community at Carrot Ranch with weekly Flash Fiction Challenges open to all writers. 99 words, no more, no less. Her mission as a literary artist is to make literary art more accessible, one flash fiction at a time.

***

PHILIP CUMBERLAND

Now retired, I have been living and working in the Cambridgeshire Fens for most of my life. Blacksmithing and wrought ironwork started as a hobby and became my profession. I have been involved in engineering in various forms all my working life.

Making things for the garden is not only an outlet for my artistic creativity, but it also helps others, garden designers and gardeners realise theirs. I am conscious that what I create, although satisfying to me in itself, will only be complete as an object when it is in place within its final setting.

Since retiring, I have joined my local University of the Third Age branch (U3A). One of the groups I belong to is Whittlesey Wordsmiths, a creative writing group. Together as a group, we have published two anthologies of our work, **Where the Wild Winds Blow** and **A Following Wind**.

With the help and encouragement of the group, I have completed my first novel, ***Killing Time in Cambridge***.

***

YVETTE PRIOR

Yvette Prior works as a university professor and conducts research. After earning a PhD in Industrial & Organizational Psychology, she poured into book projects and so far she has put together two anthologies and published four solo books.

Her past work experience has included counseling, teaching art, hospitality management, and doing outreach. Yvette finds refreshment from yoga, exploring the arts, and blogging at priorhouse.wordpress.com.

***

WENDY FLETCHER

Wendy Fletcher is the group leader of the Whittlesey Wordsmiths, a u3a (university of the third age) creative writing group.

Her first book, *The Railway Carriage Child* (available from Amazon), is a memoir of her childhood in the Cambridgeshire Fens, growing up in two Great Eastern Railway carriages. Wendy now gives talks about this to local groups.

She is currently working on a first novel as well as collecting memories and pictures to compile a social history of the small community in which she lived as a child. Her poetry has been published in *The Poet* (Christmas 2020), and you will find more poems and stories in anthologies from the Whittlesey Wordsmiths. Wendy is also the editor of the magazine of the local u3a and an occasional writer for *The Fens* magazine.

***

GLORIA MCBREEN

Gloria McBreen was born and reared with her four brothers in Bailieborough, Co Cavan. Some of her fondest memories were formed during her childhood in the Drumbannon neighbourhood. She currently resides in Ballina, Co Mayo, with her husband and youngest child. She is surrounded by inspiration, with the River Moy on her doorstep and a stunning view of Mount Nephin. She is just a short distance from dipping her toes in the Atlantic Ocean.

***

K.L. CALEY

K.L. Caley is the cliché writer…

She had known she wanted to be a writer since she was around seven years old. She remembers the first story she ever wrote.

She has read through many genres of novels, all of which have inspired her in their own ways. Her blog helps her enhance her skills, inspire creative thinking, and, perhaps more importantly, keep her in the habit of writing regularly.

She also hopes to inspire others on her writing journey. She has a few pages particularly aimed at helping and inspiring others on her blog, New2Writing.

***